VINT.

THE BLACK MAGIC WOMEN

Moushumi Kandali is a bilingual short story writer, art historian and translator. She has published four collections of short stories in Assamese, and her stories have been published in anthologies such as *The Oxford Anthology of Writings from North-East India*, *A Game of Chess: Classic Assamese Stories* and *The Greatest Assamese Stories Ever Told*. She has received several awards for creative writing, including the Bharatiya Bhasha Parishad Yuva Puraskar and Eka Ebong Koyekjon Sahitya Sanskriti Samman. She has translated Salvador Dali's autobiography into Assamese, and Miching tribal oral poetry into English. Her forthcoming book is on the modernist discourse in the visual art of Assam. Kandali taught at the School of Culture and Creative Expressions, Ambedkar University, Delhi, for several years before joining as a faculty member in the department of cultural studies in Tezpur Central University.

Parbina Rashid is a senior journalist with the *Tribune*. She has translated a number of books from the Assamese into English, including *Painting of the Sky and Other Stories*, *Ballad of Kaziranga*, *If a River and Other Stories* and *Echoes from the Valley*. Rashid has been associated with Sahitya Akademi, Delhi, in the capacity of a translator and editor. She hails from Guwahati and is based in Chandigarh.

ADVANCE PRAISE FOR THE BOOK

'Here is a bunch of exceptionally powerful stories that work at many semantic planes and reveal the range of Moushumi Kandali's concerns as a writer. Moushumi deals boldly, yet suggestively with social and political questions. Her handling of the erotic is mature, her symbolism fresh, her style enchantingly lyrical and profoundly meditative. Here is the new voice of Indian fiction, daring, philosophical, intensely poetic'—K. Satchidanandan, poet, critic and winner of the Sahitya Akademi award

'This is the unspoken part of womanhood. This series of stories read like a mix of thrillers, poetry and song lyrics. Moushumi Kandali captures a side of the North-east that, while lushly rendered as remote and exotic, rings universal to the human condition, its suffering and survival'—S. Mitra Kalita, author, columnist, media executive and winner of the Pulitzer Prize

The Black Magic Women

Moushumi Kandali

Translated by Parbina Rashid

VINTAGE
An imprint of Penguin Random House

VINTAGE

USA | Canada | UK | Ireland | Australia
New Zealand | India | South Africa | China

Vintage is part of the Penguin Random House group of companies
whose addresses can be found at global.penguinrandomhouse.com

Published by Penguin Random House India Pvt. Ltd
4th Floor, Capital Tower 1, MG Road,
Gurugram 122 002, Haryana, India

First published in Vintage by Penguin Random House India 2022

10 9 8 7 6 5 4 3 2 1

ISBN 9780143451105

Typeset in Adobe Caslon Pro by MAP Systems, Bengaluru, India

www.penguin.co.in

To the women of the North-east and the world . . .

Contents

The Black Magic Women

Assam Desh, 25 August 1835

John McCosh sahib's face was like a pale stone. In the light of the fire made by burning dried nahar seeds, those sapphire eyes were as mysterious as those of a black king cobra twinkling in the dark.

McCosh sahib was suffering from heartburn. What magic potion had that enchantress given him? He poured a little gin into a tall earthen jar. Deer meat and silkworm fry were being roasted in two other earthen pots nearby.

Captain Janikson had sent a housekeeper and a servant with household goods needed for McCosh's makeshift house—from an embroidered mattress to a cane box, a pruning knife to dazzling metallic bowls to pitchers—but McCosh sahib poured his drink into the earthen jar. The taste of gin and the flavour of the vessel blended together and danced in his mouth. Each drop of his blood jumped rhythmically—gin gin gin gin gite, te tak te, taginita . . . gin gin . . . ahh! The blood carried the fire to every pore of his body, even as the flame fuelled by the nahar seeds started to fade. Bringing a seed from the basket kept handy, he picked up a long bamboo stick and stuck the seed into its far end. The fire started once again, and his heart lit up bright as well. You, black magic woman, what did you feed me in the afternoon?

The aroma of the burnt earth of this part of the globe mingled with the exotic taste from a faraway country, burning into his consciousness. His tongue, engulfed by that fire, started muttering,

'To James Ranken
Dear Sir,
My report will be ready soon. I will be submitting to you the strange census undertaken by the Statistics Department under the administration of Her Majesty and the Company. However, sir, I feel as though an angel or a witch or a river spirit has put a spell on me, my mind is not in my control. I...I...'

The white sahib collapsed.

He managed to drag himself to his curved wooden bed, and as he lay there, he could hear her giggles. She had said, 'Sahib, this type of fever cannot be cured with a herbal medicine pack on the head and a monster leech on the body. Even if a monster leech sucks your hot blood out for seven days and seven nights, this cursed fever of yours will not recede. Are you listening to the sound of the *kalghanta* bell? Your time is ticking away.'

* * *

Hearing the beating of the drum in the middle of the night, McCosh sahib broke into a cold sweat. Getting up from the bed, he started towards the window secured by bamboo grills. Opening it slightly, he looked outside. It was just the sound of the *Dala ghata, Banti pura* rituals.

A strange custom of this strange country, hunting in the middle of the night while sailing on a boat. Opening the door, the sahib came out to the courtyard. He saw, against the current of the overflowing Pagala river, a boat, a *buti* or *selengi* boat, moving slowly, keeping close to the bank. Standing on the concave heart of the boat were three shadowy figures. The one standing in front, closest to the mast, was holding a burning torch. Behind him was another man, holding a cymbal and beating it hard. Behind him was the third man, holding a spear.

Spellbound by the illusion created by the light and the rhythmic sound, a herd of deer would approach the boat from land or a shoal of huge garua, bargala, bami and bahpati fish would charge towards the boat, and the spear would pierce through their heart. Dala ghata, Banti pura. Rhythmic sound, blazing fire. Sound and fire, fire and sound. Does the fire dance to the rhythm of the cymbal or is the cymbal's rhythm dictated by the dancing fire?

A lyrical and mysterious scene, enthralling yet fear-inducing. A shiver went down McCosh sahib's spine.

The heartrending cry of a deer cut through the night. The boat picked up speed.

Makshe sahib, that's what the locals called the man who had travelled across seven seas and thirteen rivers, finally arriving in this part of the country on a similar boat from Calcutta.

The first half of his journey was in a huge wooden craft with a sail, and later on a rowboat. Those oar-propelled boats were usually used for carrying soldiers and inland letters and parcels. In one of those overcrowded vessels, he had reached Pandu Ghat.

Sailing in the huge river for days, he was fascinated by the many moods of the river. The river never looked like a river, it looked like an ocean. They said it was a male river, the son of Brahma, the creator of the universe. In this land, even the rivers were male or female.

His journey continued on elephant back. In the towns, he travelled in a horse-drawn coach provided by the Commissioner, Captain Jackson. Jackson had supplied him with all the necessary documents needed to carry out the survey: A mine of information collected by Mr Scott, Buchanan and other locals and written by hand. Looking at the treasure trove of knowledge and data, he was ecstatic. How many articles would he now be able to send to the *Asiatic Society Journal* or to the medical science journals for publication!

Like a true-blue adventurer, travelling by boat, elephant, horse and, at times, on foot, he was constantly on the lookout for new truths and discoveries. Starting from Pandu, travelling hundreds of miles upwards, he had reached the final point of the landmass. During his journey from the lower part of the state to the upper region, which stretched from the foothills of the Patkai range to the Himalayas, he felt as if he was in an art gallery. One painting after another, each frame filled with a variety of colours, rhythms, forms and beauty.

The bag of notebooks on his shoulders was growing heavier. On his lithography slates, the figures and forms were presenting themselves in myriad ways—the banks of the Brahmaputra, earrings, *dul* pendants, moupiya birds, dancing birds or looms, textiles, utensils, bows and arrows, herbs, flowers from the unknown wilderness. With the hands of an amateur lithographer and his wanderlust-sharpened mind, he captured many aspects of life here—the people, history, culture, nature, folklore. What he was most curious about was the local *Kabiraji* way of practising medicine, and the ways of the witch doctors with their wry smiles. Moving around these areas, he was sniffing out these practices.

After all, he himself was a medical practitioner.

On the trail of one such case, he had reached the gates of a rickety hut. He had wanted to observe a doctor practising the local medicine and, possibly, try his hand at it too. By the time he returned, he was infected with a strange virus which made him listless. His body trembled from a nameless fever. The trembles had begun the moment he set foot in the compound. He was a well-built man too, this robust McCosh sahib!

From the gate he could assess that it was a poor household. The roof, which had seen better days, was now a cluster of dry grass and the cane walls were equally worn out. The man lying on a bamboo bed was a mere skeleton. He had no clothing except for a loincloth at the waist.

'Hey, bring a cloth and cover this trembling body,' the witchdoctor shouted at someone. He put a cold water-soaked cloth on the man's head.

McCosh, playing the skilful assistant to the doctor, dug out a dry leafy packet from the pocket of his baggy trousers and took out elephant leeches to release over the trembling body. The leeches, it was believed, would suck the infected blood and detoxify the body.

A woman, with a figure similar to idols made of burnt terracotta, appeared in front of him. Her chest was covered with a green bustier. She wore a traditional red embroidered *mekhela* that reached her knees. Her bare arms shone like ivory even in the darkness. She was carrying a large cloth to cover the patient.

She was surprised to find him there, but without any inhibition or fear, she stood close to her sick father. The sahib observed her with admiration—such a poor woman, but what a regal aura! The moment he set his awestruck eyes on that aura, the terracotta figurine turned into a monster elephant leech and started sucking the blood from his heart. In all honesty, she had been sucking his blood for quite some time. The leech was becoming plumper, and he was getting paler by the day. He was ready to surrender.

* * *

He had reached this place after travelling a long distance on foot, while the sun scorched the ground. People were reeling under the heat. The vigorous sahib too was exhausted. Resting for a while under an elephant-apple tree, as he was pouring a little sugarcane juice along with some homemade liquor from an earthen pot, his glazed eyes saw a wave of reapers with bare arms and bare calves, holding shiny sickles, coming out of a paddy field. They looked like a group of colourful butterflies hovering around the greens. Sahib was bewildered. He had never witnessed something like this before. He had seen many female bonded labourers at work in several places in this huge land. Never before had he seen a group of women so alive and energetic, laughing and chatting among themselves without fear or hesitation. With broken sentences in the local language, he asked them, 'What are these tools for, would you explain?'

They did not stop out of imposed modesty, nor did they become coquettish and flee, nor did they pull the veil over their face and keep mum following the dictum that a woman should not talk to a strange man. Rather, using gestures, they responded quite naturally—they did not have the time to chat. However, one sweet face among them smiled and gestured— follow us. After following them for a short distance, she pointed at a beautifully carved house with a lush garden and instructed him to go inside.

Inside McCosh met the witchdoctor, Ujha Manmath. Though the witchdoctor was from the lower part of the state, he had made the upper part of the land, nestling at the foothills of Patkai, his home. The royal family there had entrusted his forefathers to carry out prayers and rituals. He would visit his native place once a while. Whenever he went on a pilgrimage it was either out of the state to the faraway ghats of the Holy River or to pay obeisance to Goddess Bagala atop the sacred hill Nilachal Kamakhya, near the majestic river of his native place, the same river which had brought John McCosh to the shore of this land.

After a few days, as per the instructions of the good doctor, the sahib made a temporary shelter at this secluded place close to the river. Along with him were a servant and a housekeeper carrying the goods Captain Jackson had sent. On one side of his temporary home was a vast expanse of green fields stretching as far as the eyes could see and beyond that was a deep jungle that reached a range of hills creating an undulating terrain with its high peaks and deep valleys.

On the other side flowed the turbulent Pagala river. Nestled in this vast beauty was the village that kept chuckling like a healthy child. The sahib was unaware that the child sometimes cried with hunger and often slept after being fed opium.

One day, waking from an opium-induced sleep, the sahib heard a strange noise. It was rhythmic, followed by some melodious notes. In women's voices. The music was so pleasing that the sahib, mesmerized, started towards its source. He reached the huge banyan tree in the middle of the field and stood there bewildered, like a cow bitten by a snake. It was the women from the paddy fields. They were dancing in a circle playing a musical bamboo instrument. In gay abandon, they hooted and swayed to the melodious song. They seemed to be in a trance, as if they had consumed liquor. Adding another note to their music, some birds, either a cuckoo or a keteki, cooed hauntingly. The combined melody tied him to the spot. Among those women, the sahib saw that bewitching face as well, whirling like a top, creating a surreal web. The curves of her body started sucking on his heart like hundreds of elephant leeches. His throat had gone dry with a thirst that could not be quenched.

Noticing his red eyes when he returned home at dawn, his housekeeper, with knowing eyes, said to the servant, 'I hope he has not gone crazy, seeing those women dancing Bihu the whole night.' The servant replied, 'It's time he is taken to Mayong. The black magic women of Mayong can shoot their enchanted arrows and turn him into a lamb. He need not go back to the mainland or back to his white country. Let him remain here as a lamb.' They chuckled. Hearing the word Mayong, the sahib smiled to himself and thought, 'Why does anybody need to go to Mayong? This part of the country has witches everywhere. All of them are black magic women.' Did not one of them just tear his heart apart with a deadly arrow? The enchantress who had first alighted from the green field in the afternoon and then danced Bihu in the middle of night? At midday, looking like a terracotta figurine, she had appeared in the dark, dingy hut, which was illuminated with her presence, and instantly turned into an elephant leech.

* * *

After spending a few minutes with the patient, John McCosh was leaving the dingy room. Kabiraj was walking ahead of him. Outside, McCosh sahib saw the sky was overcast with dense clouds and, like a sharp spear, a streak of lightning cut across the sky. The song of the doikala bird was arousing and growing intense. What was the ethereal voice calling out from behind, a thousand times more melodious than the doikala?

Looking back, he saw her. That terracotta doll. She was beckoning him back into the hut. As he reached the courtyard, she joined both hands and stretching out before him like one does before God, she bowed her head. John McCosh was bewildered. Not knowing what he was expected to do, he looked at her helplessly. He noticed a dark green leaf in her palms. The shape of the leaf was that of a heart. Sahib was startled. The leaf silently conveyed to him a thousand meanings. On that leaf was a small fruit, cut into two equal halves. Amidst the web of intricate patterns on the fruit was a spot of white. Spellbound, he gazed at the betel nut and paan and, accepting the offerings, he put it in his mouth.

The sharp secretions from that exotic paan wreaked havoc on his unaccustomed tongue. It overpowered him, he felt as if a drum was beating wildly inside his chest, capsizing his heart. His ears grew hot, droplets of sweat appeared on his forehead and his pulse rate soared. Seeing his condition, she grabbed a ball of jaggery and thrust it into his mouth. Oh ho, sahib, you are not yet used to having raw betel nut and paan like us, right? She offered him a brass bowl filled with soothing cold water.

He recalled what Kabiraj had told him the other day, after the night he had watched the Bihu dance. He had explained to him the suggestive meaning of Bihu and the symbolic gesture of a *bihuwan*, the long white silk-cotton cloth with red flowers on the border, which the women weave with their wooden handlooms. The wise Kabiraj had revealed to him the secret behind the tune of Bihu, which was full of indicative meanings of offering betel nuts and paan.

However, the betel nut and paan the terracotta doll had offered him was nothing but a token of gratitude for a godsend witchdoctor.

Reeling under that burning sensation, as he was recalling the juicy words coming from the expert narrator, the respected one, sahib couldn't see the dichotomy of the narrative. The weather was disturbing, the clouded sky cut through by frequent lightning. The doikala bird was cooing hauntingly at regular intervals. Moreover, he had been engrossed these days in reading the emerging poets of Romanticism and the latter's overwhelming reverberations among the literati in his faraway country. These ideas came down like sudden torrential rain over his dazed soul on this exotic afternoon and gave birth to an obscure sensitivity. Seeped in that intense feeling, his soul did not allow him to sleep in peace. With a restless soul, he was now standing in his backyard, watching the primitive way of hunting and fishing by beating drums and burning torches. Dala ghata, Banti pura.

The arrow that pierced through the heart of the deer injured his heart too. It was a hunt carried out by creating a deceptively beautiful illusion with rhythmic sound and bright light. McCosh sahib went back inside. He poured the remainder of the jar of Beefeater Gin down his throat. Burning another nahar seed, he opened the notebook lying on his camp *khat*. Sitting on a wooden *maisa*, using a tall wooden stool for a table, he started writing the findings of his survey.

Just as he started to scribble in the notebook, he thought of something and closed the book. He absentmindedly rubbed the knife used to sharpen pencils on the leg of the stool, making his feather pen and inkpot shake. The sahib too was shaking inside. There was a fierce battle going on inside, between his brain and his heart. His heart said, 'She is not a deceiver. She is a real woman made of flesh and blood. A simple, independent, free-spirited woman, the way nature made her, hitherto unseen, unknown in any other part of the world. She and her ilk. Perhaps she is a representative of a handful of women in the world who are not bound by tradition or forcefully subjected to a defined system. She is not a water spirit or some divine angel. She is a human. A woman who can complement a man as his equal.'

However, John McCosh was also a man. Like every man, he too could visualize a woman only in two extreme avatars—either a pure, virtuous goddesses or a witch or enchantress. No man can accept that a woman can have both virtues and vices.

John McCosh's brain kept hammering, 'She is an enchantress. She is a huntress. She is unrestrained. She is a seductress. There is not a single grain of morality in her.'

McCosh was wearing a coat of Victorian morality. Knowingly or unknowingly, most men cover themselves in that coat all the time. This was why Kabiraj had explained to him, 'Do not befriend these low caste women who dance at night. Why did you go to watch the Bihu dance? One can never vouch for those uncultured, footloose and fancy-free women. Our upper-class royal women are different, they are very wise. You must have heard of Queen Phuleswari Kuwari? Have you written down all the information about her in your notebook? There was another warrior called Mula Gabharu. There was Jaimati, a pure virtuous woman. There were women who wrote poetry. I would still say— beware of women. Whatever class and caste she may be— beware! Nobody can tell what a *tiri*, a woman, is plotting. Our women know black magic. The old name of our country is Kamrup and our women were called Mohini . . . Did you get it? Have you, by the way, visited the Madan Kamdev Peeth, the sacred temple of our god of lust and love? It is just a little way away from the capital. Go and visit, you will find plenty of inspiration for painting.'

The wise one had chuckled. He was a well-read and well-informed witchdoctor. Due to his wisdom, the people had accorded him the status of the village head. This wise old man's advice made a lasting imprint on sahib's mind. Everywhere in this world, the way men think is more or less the same. After all, it is a world of men, by men and for men. Isn't it, O, wise one? In every battle between the heart and the brain, the brain always wins. That night, once again, the heart had lost the battle. The night let out a howl like the injured deer. The sahib stopped pacing. He sat down once again at the wooden stool. He picked up his notebook and feather pen. Compiling the report for the Company, he started writing.

'The women of this country, they form a striking contrast to the men. They are very fair, indeed fairer than any other race I have seen in India. Radiantly fair. Many of them would be considered beautiful. I do not mean Hindostani beauty, but the Assamese women have a form and feature closely approaching the European. In parts of the country not frequented by Europeans, the women roam about in public divested of the artificial modesty practised by native ladies in other parts of India. Unfortunately, their morality is at a low ebb. The inhabitants of most provinces look down upon the Assamese as enchanters, and the women come in for a large share of suspicion—indeed, they all are believed to be enchantresses.'

As he wrote, John McCosh kept murmuring, 'Yes, they all are black magic women. They are.'

* * *

Delhi, 25 August 2015

> Got a black magic woman,
> I've got a black magic woman,
> Got me so blind I can't see,
> That she's a black magic woman,
> She's trying to make a devil outta me.

She was reading a book and listening to Santana. She felt good listening to this song. Since she had shifted to this new residential area, she had been feeling quite herself. In the easternmost part of the national capital, this was a colony surrounded by tall walls, CCTV cameras and with security guards at the entrance. No unwanted elements could enter here. There were pavements for pedestrians and beautiful gardens dotted the whole complex. Much to her relief, judging by the way they dressed and spoke, this was a considerably cosmopolitan colony.

Before she moved here, she'd lived in the older part of the city, which appeared to live in medieval times. The place fell along the state boundary and was prone to crime and smuggling. The area proudly announced its identity as the largest Chor Bazaar, chock-a-block with stolen goods. A few lanes away, crossing a vast barren land, was a garden named after some Dilshad. Who was this Dilshad, she often wondered. Every time she walked through it, she was filled with frustration and sadness. It was not Dilshad but *Dil* Sad. A saddened heart.

The roads echoed with sarcastic laughter and abuses filled with sexual innuendos, hungry eyes always on the lookout for prey. The ugly words and laughter had become a norm.

She recalled seeing a huge crowd near the slaughterhouse in the market. She had stopped out of curiosity. A woman in the crowd told her, 'It's nothing much. A nine-year-old is lying there. She had been missing for the past two days. Somebody was in heat.'

She was shocked at the way that woman spoke. Over time, she had observed that such ugly, unnatural things were accepted as normal, while things that should go unnoticed got people's antennas up.

One day she had found herself at the receiving end of their curious antennas. She had ventured into a Saturday market, which reminded her of the Sunday markets at the tea estate from her childhood. As a wave of nostalgia washed over her, like a newly born calf, she ran towards the hazy by-lanes from the past. How enticing the fares were, from colourful balloons, ribbons and terracotta toys to chickpea fries and puffed rice, from plastic bangles and hairclips to ornate calendars of a girl holding a rose and saying namaste. She was a child again looking here and there, at this and that, not knowing what to buy and what not. From Kolhapuri chappals to knives and pans! From blingy dupattas to hot jalebis! She was Alice, moving on the colourful lanes of Wonderland. She ventured further in to buy an aluminium kettle and a few ladles. Suddenly, she felt like she was being attacked by thousands of eyes from every direction. On the surface, nothing was wrong, but something was terribly amiss.

Surveying her surroundings, she realized it was an area meant only for men. In long kurtas, *surma*-smeared eyes and netted skullcaps, she could see only the silhouettes of male bodies. There were women as well, but only a few, facelessly in the shadow of the male figures. A black robe covered them from head to toe. With their eyes, their only live feature, they were pleading with her silently—Go back. Go back home. Don't hover around this place like a butterfly. Go back sister, go back home.

A male voice struck her like an arrow, '*Mohtarma, dhang ke kapre pehna kijiye. Akele mat ghumiye. Shyam ke bad toh sirf dayanein hi nikalti hain.* You should not be out in the evening, and that too so indecently clothed.'

How strange is this metropolis; here, a 'village' called Hauz Khas that boasts of nightlife like Paris coexists with this place. Here you are taunted because you are wearing a pair of jeans and walking alone in the evening. In a huff, she turned back and, like a flying snake that glides through the air, she jumped on the first rickshaw she saw, still panting.

When she had regained her composure, the rickshaw-wallah asked her, '*Beti*, why did you go to that market alone, without a male escort? That marketplace is not frequented by our people you know; it is their area, don't you see? Don't you hear every day how they scream on top of their voices, that too into a mic, five times a day, tearing the sky and our ears apart? On top of that, you are dressed in English clothes. Pants and shirt. Don't mind. It's just fatherly advice.' Dropping her off in front of her rented apartment, he added a parting shot, 'See there is a temple just across. You should be going there. Do you ever go there? Go there every day, at least every Monday, okay? All marriageable girls should pray to Shivji. Shivji will fulfil your wishes. The priests in the temple campus will protect you if necessary. God bless you, beti.'

For the first time, she looked at the temple with interest. A temple made of colourful shiny tiles. Each tile contained a blue image of Shiva holding a trident. She couldn't find the grace and beauty of the stone-cut ancient temples in her native place. There was a strange song, 'Jai Bholebaba', continuously playing on loudspeakers. Strange, because the tone of the bhajan was based on a popular Hindi song—*Mere sapno ki rani kab aayegi tu—Mere sapno ka Bholebaba kab aayega tu* . . . She imagined Shiva's blue visage in a Rajesh Khanna dance, shaking his head for no rhyme or reason! Whenever she would try to meditate on Shiva, Rajesh Khanna's clownish movement would overpower her vision, leaving no space for imagination or meditation. This confluence appeared tasteless. Wouldn't it be a better idea to lie on the bed and read the verses by some Virashaiva saints or some Andal poetess or some Therigathas or some Sufi saints and attain spiritual fulfilment, like a cow which chews the cud calmly in the night at the cowshed? What about Rumi's divine verses which carry a deep meaning beyond words? How beautifully an ethereal rhythm strings those words together.

However, the last resort for people suffering from worldly woes, the temple which had provided so many a ray of hope, couldn't be ignored. Every morning as she stepped out to collect her newspapers from the gate, she would throw a curious glance at the temple. Early in the morning even God seemed to be at peace. A few meditative monkeys would welcome the morning, and the hopping squirrels would declare the dawn in glee. The day felt like it would pass peacefully.

On one such calm morning, she saw five men walking towards her gate. Red *tilaks* marked their foreheads. Colourful threads adorned their wrists and *rudrakshas* hung around their necks. They made her uneasy. They barged into her house and before she could say anything, one of them with a baritone voice ordered her, 'Pay some respect to God, Madamji. Give Rs 5000 for Mata's *jagaran*.' In front of the five domineering men, she did not know what to do. Two of them had walked past the living area and were peeping into her bedroom, saying, 'You live alone. You should worship God, he will protect you.' Those adamant men with their sinister laughter extracted Rs 3000 from her. Before leaving, one of them with tobacco-stained teeth said to her, 'Give us your mobile number. We can ensure your well-being. We have heard about the

Kamakhya temple at your native place and that black magic is practised over there. Mysterious things happen there during the Ambovachi mela. Do you also know any black magic Madamji, *kuch jadu tona*? Hahaha . . . don't kill us, ok?'

Who was killing whom, bit by bit?

She was not one to be cowed. True, a few bitter experiences had painted dark circles under her eyes, but she was still in control, she knew how to sit behind the steering wheel of life and change gears. Like Mr Gogol in *The Namesake*, her name too had become a burden. Axomi. Why was she christened with that name? Her colleagues teased her by calling her Asami, a criminal. Sometimes she thought she indeed was an *asami*, imprisoned in her uniqueness, the way she talked, the way she dressed, the way she behaved and, most importantly, the way she looked. Why didn't she have a location-neutral, culture-neutral name? Despite this, she was in control of her life. She could fully enjoy the dialogues of the plays by Manto or Chughtai, the evergreen *Mrcchakatika* staged at Mandi House, the passionate bargaining amidst the cacophony at Sarojini Nagar market or Lajpat Nagar bazaar, the haunting *kalbelia* tunes played at the courtyard of Dilli Haat and the experimental art in the rows of galleries at Lado Sarai.

Friends came over and played fusion tunes with their guitars. She tasted chakli and litti-chokha with them and, on Christmas Eve, she hung a shining star on her door. A lone star. It twinkled in the anarchic surroundings. The very next day she had to face a volley of questions, 'Star? Why are you putting up a star? Who are you? Where are you from? Religion? Caste? If you are not a Christian, then why are you putting up a star, you crazy woman? Look, this is not your native place where you can do whatever you like, even dance naked; here we have culture, great culture and tradition.'

Without losing control over the gears, she drove the car of her life. She thought, 'This is only a reflection of the thick polluted air that blows daily in this city. There must be a pure breeze blowing somewhere. There must be some place somewhere in this ancient, beautiful city where you can relax in your courtyard, even if it is a rented one, and gaze at the stars which sometimes look like pearls and sometimes wounds on the chest of the sky.'

The cemented backyard of her rented house, nestled in the underbelly of the city, was barricaded by the walls of three buildings. Between the gaps of the bricks grew a few Pipal trees and a yellow creeper. She used to dry her clothes in the backyard and when she went to collect them after returning from work, she would often gaze at the small square of sky available to her, the twinkling stars winking at her from a velvety black sky. How familiar they looked. They seemed to be calling out to her as they winked. Stretching out her hands, she would sway at the spot. Once, as she was looking up at the sky, she saw something falling. What was it? A shooting star? Nah. A small packet landed next to her. In the darkness she could not make out what it was. The next morning the cover of the packet revealed its contents. Repulsed, she picked it up and threw it in the dustbin, the hidden meaning of that packet assaulting her sensibility. More such packets came her way at frequent intervals and one day, it took an ugly turn when the suggestive gesture, instead of coming down as an empty packet, took the shape of an inflated balloon. A small transparent pink balloon, filled with a semi-liquid substance called semen.

This time the balloon took the shape of a snail and, leaving a trail of slime behind, came towards her to gobble her.

Just a few days later, carrying her belongings in an auto-van, she moved into a flat in the residential colony with CCTV cameras and alert guards with a register to note down the names of anyone who desired to enter this castle. As she unlocked her flat with the cartons of her belongings, her books and CDs, she felt good, like stepping on a lush green garden after spending days in a stinking toilet without water or fresh air.

The flat had been arranged for by a few of her acquaintances. They were permanent residents of the colony which had roughly thirty multi-storied apartments, ten flats on each floor. Opening the window, she saw a row of deodar trees, a few green conical yearnings rising towards the sky. Colourful kites dotted the sky. A flock of sparrows and cormorants flew about, and piercing the air was the cry of a peacock. Harsh but beautiful as it carried the promise of a golden-blue beauty. It felt magical.

She played the song 'Black Magic Woman'. The deep baritone filled her room, 'I got a black magic woman . . .' She looked at her watch. 11 p.m. She did not feel like having dinner. In the evening, catching up with her friends at the green courtyard of the Press Club, they had wiped out the snack plates. The memory made her smile. It was so much fun spending time with her girlfriends, like getting on the bus to go on her first-ever picnic. The conversation as always ventured into the same old premise. Someone was a lecturer, someone an NGO worker, someone worked at a call centre and someone worked for a corporate house. The organizer of their get-togethers was a busy newspaper reporter.

They worked in different fields, had different experiences and thrills, but in one particular area they all could relate to one another as if they were all sailing on the same boat. No, not fellow passengers of a boat but inmates of the same prison. They all wore the same uniform. A uniform which was thrust upon them. A uniform woven with set stereotypes and fantasies about an unknown exotic land and its people with a distinct look and way of life. The women in this uniform talked and shared their tales, munching peanuts and chicken fry in the open lawn.

Somebody was offered a lift by her colleague on her way back home. Seeing a familiar face, she had trustingly got into his car. Another one, seeing her colleagues having lunch at the canteen, walked up to them and occupied the empty chair. Someone else broke out in laughter while standing close to a colleague. These are a few snapshots from routine life, but this normal behaviour becomes offensive while it gets distorted by accusing fingers. Everyone was awarded with adjectives—cheap, easy, loose, available, asking-for-it types. Slut, seductress, enchantress. Surprisingly, they got such names from their own acquaintances and companions, their friends and familiar ones, not from some stranger.

Sharing and talking about all these, they would feel like a patient who was not properly anesthetized before the surgery. They felt the nausea, lying inert and dizzy, stuck on an operation table in a frosty room. The entire world felt like a sick world which had never seen women or women like them.

'I have never seen a woman like you in the entire world, Suzanne,' as if Leonard Cohen was addressing her in his song. This song was dedicated to Suzanne. She felt like

Suzanne, she felt happy listening to this song. After Santana, she started humming Cohen's song.

> Suzanne takes you down to her place near the river,
> You can hear the boats go by,
> You can spend the night beside her ...
> And just when you mean to tell her,
> That you have no love to give her,
> She gets you on her wavelength,
> And she lets the river answer,
> That you've always been her lover,
> And you want to travel with her ...

Listening to the song she thought, 'Really? Was there a man in this world who would go away on an unknown trail with a woman by his side?' As if to answer her question, at 11.15 p.m., the phone rang.

A familiar voice. He had never called this late before. In the background other voices could be heard. And laughter. He was not alone. He admitted that he was enjoying a few drinks with his friends. She asked anxiously, 'Why did you call so late? There must be something important.' He broke out in a throaty laughter and said, 'Nothing much. Just called to find out how you are doing. You live so far away, God knows what you would be doing. What a life, man! Good for you. You are leading a charmed life. You are really enjoying life. What say? We were just talking about you. Our historian was saying, "What to say about these Kamrup women? They know black magic." How many people have you cast your spell on?'

The historian friend snatched the phone from his hand and said, 'By the way, have you watched the news? One magic woman from your country has sent the entire country into a tizzy. What a horrendous crime she has committed.'

She had watched the evening news, the national channels as well as the regional ones. She had seen the woman, Indrajaya, who had sent the country into a tizzy. She had seen the result of an alleged cold-blooded murder. The most heinous crime a mother could commit: killing her own child. But was it the general norm? If what was being shown on TV was the truth, it was an exception. Someone had gone astray.

Why should every woman from her land bow her head in shame? In a bloodied script of consumerism and greed for power, it was an extreme epilogue, fit to be a case study for psychologists.

She thought of the honour killings that took place every day. How parents snuffed out the life of their children in the name of the honour of their clan. She thought of incidents where parents killed their newborn daughters by stuffing salt into their mouth or while she was still in her mother's womb. The Indrajaya incident had turned into a melodramatic play. A high-profile entertaining thriller for the upper echelon of society.

As television channels fought for bytes, most women in the panel discussions roared in animated, fierce verbosity, trying to justify themselves to the world, 'Listen, I love my child, I go out for work, but my top priority is my child and my family.' Is there a woman who does not think of her child as her everything? Why were they trying so hard to prove their stand? Were they suffering from some persecution complex? Were they scared that they too would be included in the Indrajaya category? We are ashamed, really ashamed, we are not like her.

One man mocked, '*Arre yaar, yeh hai* women liberation *mere bhai. Narivaad ki jai ho.*' Another one started in a meditative stance, 'This is what they do for money, honey-trapping. They prey on business tycoons with their charm and beauty, these modern-day enchantresses and seductresses, like the ancient *apsaras* seducing the saints and *nagarbadhus* and trapping the kings and generals.'

As the TRPs soared, people sat on their couch engrossed, some cursed and lamented at the fall of the free modern woman, some laughed at the marvellous spectacle unfolding on the screen before them, some poured more drinks into their glasses and some like this historian and his sophisticated Mayo-bred CEO friend made this call to her, teasing her 'just in banter' that Indrajaya had carried forward her legacy by performing black magic on that old business tycoon, who had fallen for her mesmerizing charm and turned into a lamb. They asked her if she too had similar plans. 'Just joking. Don't all the women from your place perform black magic, especially those women from Mayong, don't they turn a man into a lamb? You too are a black magic woman, right?' They laughed and repeated, 'Just in banter, just in banter . . .'

Keeping the phone down, she thought, ugh, there is no escape. Just when she had thought that she could breathe easy. One thing remained constant, the way you will be looked at. Slouching down at the washbasin, she spat. Filling the mug with water, she splashed it on the wall. The wet portion of the wall looked like a huge mushroom. Like a mushroom cloud.

She picked up two books from her bookshelf. The first was a report, which she had found in the library of a research institute. She had chanced upon the photocopy of the report of a land survey as she was flipping through some historical documents. The man who had compiled it was John McCosh. The statistics was compiled for the Company, addressed to Sir James Ranken. The date of submission was 14 June 1837. Reading the long comment on pages 22 and 23, she was shocked. It was about the women of her region.

'The women of this state are beautiful but practise black magic. As they mingle with people freely, they are morally loose. They are enchantresses.'

She was speechless.

She recalled another comment from the medieval era. A comment that stemmed from a similar observation made through the patriarchal lens, from the king of Gaud, Shaista Khan, to Ram Singh.

Ram Singh was a general in Aurangzeb's army, the son of Jai Singh. Shaista Khan had told Ram Singh, 'Don't bring women of that country to the camp. They are beautiful enchantresses from the land of black magic.' The same thought echoed in the statement of history writer Shihabuddin Talish, a companion of Mir Jumla. From Shaista Khan to John McCosh, everyone had uttered the same words, 'Mohini, Mohini . . . the black magic women . . .'

She opened the second book, and a smile touched her lips. She turned to a particular page of the huge volume. A poem that spread from page 659 to 668. She started reciting the beautiful verses, pouring her emotions into it.

I am Pragjyotika, Kamrupa, I am like the cascading stream. Every day in my heart thousands of turbulent waves of a hundred rivers of the Brahmaputra rise up and die down,

blending with the mesmerizing painting like the blue
Naga Hills.
I am the queen of nature, I am the painter, I am the creator
of this new world.
I will travel from country to country, through land and sea.
I will light up every soul in the world.

She kept reciting and her eyes welled up. Overwhelmed with
gratitude, she let her tears, crystallized with heartfelt emotions
over the years, fall. On an impulse, she picked up the phone
and called back her callers. 'Listen, it's late and you people
are drunk. Tomorrow, in the daytime, when you all sober up,
I will post a poem to you. It was written by a man like you.
Most interestingly, his forefathers had migrated from this side
of the land to our part a hundred years ago, his ancestry was
similar to yours, but they settled there and mingled, married
and assimilated with us. That man wrote this on 3 June, in
the year 1943.'

She kept the phone down and noticed another strange
coincidence. John McCosh had written the report in the
month of June. Almost a hundred years before Jyotiprasad
wrote this poem. Both of their visions were focused on women,
but what a diametrically opposite outlook. She tried to make
sense of it. Why did John McCosh write such a thing in that
report? On what grounds? Whom did he see? Whom did he
meet? On what basis had he called the women 'Black Magic
Women'? What happened to you, John McCosh? Being in
the company of elephant leeches and bitter herbs, had you
forgotten about the fragrance of gulanchi flowers?

She visualized John McCosh, imagined her predecessors
whom John McCosh had probably met on the streets.

How were they? Were they characterless just because they did not fit into the parameters of John McCosh's world? McCosh's contemporaries had termed the black African women as aggressively sensual sluts. Comparing them with upper-class European women, they had called lower-class, dark-skinned women ugly sinners. Did John McCosh do the same thing?

What about Jyotiprasad? Why did he write this poem? She knew it was a somewhat romanticized depiction. What intense urge had he felt that he had to write it, especially those two lines—'I will travel from country to country, through land and sea. I will light up every soul in the world.'

A photograph she had seen years ago in an anthology of Jyotiprasad came to her mind. A black and white picture. A boat sailing in a river, Jyotiprasad sitting on the boat. In the backdrop, a cityscape of a Western country. Perhaps Berlin, where he had trained in filmmaking. This was her favourite picture of Jyotiprasad from the printed collection of photographs in that volume, and remained etched like a metaphor in her subconscious. In her imagination, she too sailed in that boat in the cascading river that flowed into a wide horizon. In an incoherent voice, she asked him, 'Jyotiprasad, did you ever get tired? Sometimes I feel very tired. Like a water carrier, I have been carrying the bamboo stick with two heavy containers on my shoulders since time immemorial. When will the weight from our shoulders lift? Only if we could throw away the shackles of our identity as easily as we remove our brassiere before we go to sleep! We could have slept in peace forever.'

Keeping the book open over her chest and sailing along in her imaginary river, as she surrendered herself to a deep sleep, Axomi saw that she was rowing her own boat across a turbulent river. All around her was nothing but grey waves. Above her was the open sky.

As the boat rocked, she felt afraid. She looked back in apprehension. There was nothing but silence all around. She was so lonely.

Amidst that haziness, she saw another boat. On that boat was Jyotiprasad. He waved at her and his voice echoed over the turbulent waves, 'Move on, move on, keep going, don't look back. Bon voyage, bon voyage . . . '

**The character named Jyotiprasad narrated in this story refers to the real-life persona of Jyotiprasad Agarwala, the cultural doyen of Assam who was a renowned progressive writer, lyricist and aesthetician. He also made the first Assamese film, *Joymoti*, in 1934. 'I am Pragjyotika, Kamrupa, I am like the cascading stream' is the author's translation of the poem 'Axomiya Suwalir Ukti' from *Jyotiprasad Rachanavali*, edited by Dr Hiren Gohain.

The story has been written in response to a report 'Topography of Assam' by John McCosh, an assistant surgeon who submitted it to James Ranken, Esq, MD, Officiating Secretary, Medical Board, Bengal in 1835. The published report in form of a book has been archived in the library of Indian Institute of Advanced Studies, Shimla. In this book, John McCosh commented that Assamese women (Section 2, Chapter 3, Pages 22, 23) are all enchantresses with low morality who practise black magic. The monologue given at the end of the first part is a quote from this report. In 2012, while browsing through the archives with writer–journalist Sangeeta Barooah Pisharoty, we came across this report. I sincerely thank Sangeeta. This story would have not been written if you hadn't jumped in excitement and cried out, 'Hey, look at this!'

The Hyenas and
Coach Number One

For the women who migrate to the city in search of their dreams

The scar stretched from the left mound of her chest to her armpit. It resembled a knife with a crooked end. It ran deep, and a blood clot had turned black. A mouth, hungrily exploring the crevice and the mound, had left that mark. A moan often spiralled from that gash, threatening to uncoil like a hissing cobra. She suppressed that moan with a bra, a kurta and a thick coat.

The dark window of the metro coach, moving fast on the serpentine underground track, reflected her face. Her reflection got superimposed over the scenes from the platforms outside like an abstract painting—opaque, complex, layered. She stared at her reflection. A face marred with pain and the lethal vapour arising from the scar. The train was moving inside the tunnel at full speed, making a rhythmic sound. By the time it emerged from the end of the tunnel, she hopped onto the escalator and faced the world outside, the natural light replaced by what seemed to be a metallic light.

Twilight. The time when Narsimha (an avatar of Lord Vishnu) tore the asura king Hiranyakashipu to death with his long, sharp claws. A fleeting, hazy moment, that stood still between two starkly opposite realms—day and night, darkness and light, truth and lies. Like the scar on her chest, one side of which carried the soft, piercing sensuality of love and the other side, the cruel stab of lust. Could such a scar ever be erased? A scar that spread from the body and invaded her subconscious?

It was possible. Every scar of the skin could be removed. Every unwanted line, age-induced wrinkle, crow's feet—everything, if only one applied the magic cream called Olay. By applying that cream, one could turn the clock back ten years. A hoarding that touched the sky announced with conviction: Olay age-defying cream. The men at the row of small kiosks in front of the metro station selling fried groundnuts, roasted star fruits, maize and sweet potatoes, raw guavas, ripe tamarind, and running small mobile shops of Coke, chips, Tang, etc., would leer at the provocatively clad Olay model, revealing their *tiranga*-opium-tobacco-stained teeth. They would tease one another, pairing each other up with the model, conjuring obscene, despicable scenes and hooting with laughter. Whenever she climbed up the escalator and faced the outside world, she would pause, and the Olay woman would call out to her temptingly. Each time, she would resolve, this time, if that elusive bonus made its way to her bank account, she would buy that cream. Like those creatures who, flashing their *tiranga*-opium-tobacco-stained teeth, swam in the slimy ocean of primitive juices, she too, for just one moment, gave into a fantasy of a different kind. The fantasy of a flawless complexion and eternal youth.

Coming back to her senses, her racing heart in her palm, she crossed the road without a zebra crossing, with vehicles whizzing past. Aiming for her, that ancient mythical buffalo followed. With alert eyes, she looked both sides, and as she crossed the road leaving the danger behind, to seek refuge in another dark alley, she saw that the ears of the other deer too were on alert. The herd of deer that had come out of the first coach of the metro.

Yes! Every evening as she got down at the metro station on her way back from work, she remembered a scene from a documentary she had seen on Animal Planet some time back . . . It was about a herd of white-tailed deer in the rainforest. She would recall one particular scene as the women from the reserved coach hurriedly got down and ran to cross the street to go back home. The scene unfolded in her mind every time and she saw the herd of deer so vividly! With ears perked up, the herd moved towards the flowing river to quench its thirst. They moved fast. They stopped. They looked around. They tried to sense something. Their ears were erect with apprehension. They continued their journey. Long, measured, hesitant steps, ears trying to trace some impending terror, ready to bolt if necessary. So much caution, such agonizingly measured movement, just to quench their thirst! Who knew at what moment the hyenas with crooked eyes and sharp fangs would pounce on them? Everything would be over.

Like that scene, a cry for life and a mutilated body could happen here as well. The act of mutilation could happen anytime, anywhere. *Every time, everywhere.* Like this mark on her chest that mutilated a very small and simple fantasy of hers. That fantasy of applying the Olay cream to remain eternally young and beautiful. Like finding everything back home mutilated one day and becoming a migrant to this metropolis. The train which she had boarded pushed her forward as it rhymed—move on, move on, move on. To live, to quench one's thirst, one had to walk towards the flowing water body, even though some precious moments, some inescapable memories from the past numbed one's senses, at times making it impossible to move on. Even though the loneliness, which once used to be a luxury, invaded every crevice of the mind and soul, one had no alternative but to carry the weight of life like a donkey tiptoeing on a steep climb. Move on, move on, move on, no matter how dangerous the journey was, no matter how many groups of predatory hyenas were waiting at the turns, ready to pounce at the drop of a hat; like the herd of deer, with alert eyes and measured steps, one had to approach the river to quench one's thirst.

As she was walking down the dark alley, a bag of waste, hurled from the top of a multistorey building, landed at her feet. Some stinking rotten stuff flew at her. She burst out in anger. Why? Why did the old cliché of the hyena and the deer keep coming to mind? Why did the scene from Animal Planet keep playing in her mind? She could not stand that simile. Why did you need such a simile that established the equation of the predator and the prey in the food chain? Why did it have the power to entrap her? She felt as if she was being sucked into the whirlpool of the simile.

She saw everyone around her fidgeting once the darkness descended. The hyenas might attack. Let's go, let's go home.

The anxiety to be home before it was too dark. Hyenas in every nook and cranny, waiting for an opportunity. Hyenas attacked in groups. When groups of cruel, merciless hyenas came out on a hunt, they destroyed life. In this metropolis, the hyenas did not attack only at night, they jumped on some unsuspecting prey whenever the opportunity presented itself. Kids were their favourite prey. To them, life was nothing but the few heated moments of chasing and hunting, life was nothing but what was seen through their lustful eyes.

The morning newspapers were full of these stories. Everyone took them casually. 'They were in heat, that's all,' they said. Some five-year-old had come out of the gate in the morning to play. Some seventeen-year-old had come out in the afternoon to buy a red ribbon and notebooks. Some forty-year-old had gone to the temple in the evening. None of them returned home safely. The little ones were disappearing at an alarming rate. They were lured to the road of no return with just a toffee or a colourful toy. How trustingly, how happily and innocently they followed the lead.

Had she not seen such lustful eyes earlier? Such eyes were there even in the faraway world she had left behind, but those eyes did not come in groups like these did. They waited for the prey, sometimes behind secluded bamboo grooves, sometimes the deserted curve on the road and sometimes in a dark corner of a wedding. This was open, on the roads. Those rows of Dusters, Fortuners and Innovas, she knew some of them carried the hyenas, on the lookout for prey. Was it only those Dusters, Fortuners and Innovas? Were the hyenas not present even amidst those pushing the small wooden carts? They had spread among those people who carried their miserable life over their shoulders like her.

One section came out to hunt because of the arrogance and power they derived from their name and fame, others came out to avenge their painful and depressing existence. Their powerless claws would pick soft targets to show the middle finger to destiny for throwing them into the bottomless pit of poverty and oppression. This was their only way to avenge the fruitless exercises that played in their lives, day in and day out. This was the only way out from their destiny, their everyday anger and stinking despair. A despair that stinks like a rotten gutter filled with vomit and shit.

The stink from the nearby drain wafted into her room on the terrace, making her nauseous. Her small room was in utter chaos, as if a pitch-black buffalo covered with mud was sitting in a pond of anarchy. Before that fateful day, her room had not looked like this. That was the day when a chain of events beyond her imagination had unfolded and the people, who until then had thought that home was the safest place on earth, had come out on the streets.

Their eyes and face reflecting a deep anguish, they whispered about the incident that had taken place the previous night. It was like any other hunt by the hyenas, but this one had shaken them, each one feeling like a tree uprooted by a storm. In trembling voices, they had discussed how the girl was made to endure hell's fury on the floor of a moving bus by six of them. How in that cold wintry night she was lying naked on the road, covered in her own blood. Mute cars were passing by, but none of them had stopped even for a moment. Nobody had thrown a piece of cloth on her. How the rod, stained with blood, had come out along with her intestines. People had nothing to offer to her but their remorse, prayers and a new name, Nirbhaya.

She had thrown up. She was trembling. A stifled cry jolted her body every now and then. She was about to leave her room to join the crowd marching towards the protest ground of the metropolis, when she had heard a knock at her door. He was standing at her doorstep, another migrant in this city, though from a different place—everything else seemed different, strikingly different. Though she had nothing in common with this man, her heart bonded with him like a piece of camphor on fire. After he came into her life, this city to which she did not belong felt like home. The dream of spending the rest of their lives together was taking root. She felt like surrendering herself to his embrace, like a lost little girl running into her father's arms. She reached out to the fragile straw when she thought she was drowning in the river.

Her outreached hand had touched a heart that was beating wildly. It was beating in his hands. A beautiful, white pigeon. He laughed and said, 'Today is a good day. No work today. People are stuck everywhere. With this solid excuse in hand, I could make it to your *barsati*.'

He swiftly picked up the knife and, with his smile still intact, he said, 'It's a day to celebrate. I have got this aphrodisiac for you. I have managed to get this with so much trouble.'

'What? Aphrodisiac?'

'Yes, it fills the body and mind with infinite energy. With the hot blood running through the veins, the rejuvenated body can enjoy life to the point of climax . . . countless climaxes!' He spoke like a mystic monk in a Himalayan cave, with great emphasis on the word 'climax'. Flashing a naughty smile, he held her hand. Feathers from the lifeless pigeon and the smell from bloodstained hands assaulted her nostrils. He said, 'Today I will have two baby pigeons. One lying dead in my right hand and the other in my left hand—so alive, so hot! *Aye masakali masakali, udd matakali matakali . . . Udd dagar . . . Dikhlade thenga in sab ko jo udna na jane,*' he hummed the popular Bollywood song.

Singing that beautiful song, this man was getting ready to clip her wings and snuff out her heart. How was this possible? He was her last resort in these turbulent waters. He was her address in this alien city. Could that sort of a man inflict such a mark? One does not get a whiff of it, that there is a hyena hiding even inside the most familiar person. All it takes is only a stroke of infected air to awaken that sleeping hyena in him and any man can easily wring a pigeon's neck.

She sobbed silently as the pain from the cut that stretched from her armpit to the margin of her left mound kept hitting her in waves. She saw feathers all over her kitchen floor, the basin, the bucket. Lying next to her, satiated, he murmured, 'Do you know, when I go for housekeeping, especially in the rooms of foreign visitors, I taste the leftover liquor from the discarded bottles—*wah*, what taste! They make a cocktail in our hotel bar—the name is pretty interesting, The Rapist Drink. That cocktail hits at the right spot, you see. That's why it is so much in demand.' She saw a feather, a tiny one, had lodged in his hair. She recalled a scene. A scene from this city that unfolded before her once when the sun was about to set.

A man standing on the terrace of a multistorey building was calling out into the air. Against the red sky, the man was just a silhouette. The silhouette was shouting and responding to it was a flock of pigeons which came swooping down towards him. It was a mysterious, unbelievable scene. Her colleague, who was standing next to her watching the whole thing, told her that the man domesticated the pigeons by making that peculiar sound. With that sound and the feed, he could lure the birds and whenever he felt like it, he could wring their necks and turn them into an aphrodisiac. Lying on the bed, she wondered—did she also finally turn into an aphrodisiac lured by this man lying next to her in the bed?

The bed was still unkempt. Even after two months. Removing her dress, she got into her nightgown. She took a good look at herself in the mirror. The gash in her chest was still visible. Even after two months. She didn't feel like having dinner. She stood amidst the chaos in the room, then walked towards the bed. The exhaustion from the hectic day or from the chaos of her subconscious was overpowering her senses. Oblivion-weariness-paranoia played on her chaotic mind, dragging her into a complex maze . . .

In that maze of a dream she saw that she was standing at the counter of the Olay showroom and asking the salesperson for an age-enhancing cream, a cream that gave wrinkles; instead of turning the clock back by ten years, it added twenty or thirty or fifty years. As the salesperson shut the door on her face, not before telling her that the cream was not available, she saw herself standing on a foothill! Where had the showroom vanished all of a sudden and what was this hill she had been transported to? In the dream, she looked around and found that she was standing all alone on the foothill amidst a thick veil of mist. She looked up. There, standing on the peak, was Rahdoi Ligiri. She shuddered—how could she be meeting Rahdoi Ligiri in real life as she was just a character from a novel she had read long back? But Rahdoi was standing right in front of her. Rahdoi was a maidservant. Close to her were Rupsingh Subedar, the hangman, and many other faces. Rahdoi looked around her, then looked at the big river and jumped, whispering, 'Freedom . . . freedom finally.' Rahdoi, who jumped in a quest for freedom, was being dragged by those who resurrected her inert body. Following the instructions of Swami Agamananda, she remained inside the dark cave of Silaghat for ten months and ten days in a yogic posture. Finally, she came out as Krishnadasi. Wrinkled skin, hunchback, unsteady feet, she was now sixty-year-old Krishnadasi. Rahdoi Ligiri who had turned into Krishnadasi had come out from the pages of that classic novel to meet her in the dream. She realized that and exclaimed, 'Oh God! Krishnadasi!' Krishnadasi kept looking at her, flashing a mysterious smile, and then said, 'Rajanikanta, my writer, was not capable of changing the world. He could not do it. That's why he turned the beautiful young Rahdoi Ligiri into old Krishnadasi. Probably that was the only option available for Rajanikanta, to wipe out the pain, to lodge a silent protest. Why have you sent your character in search of the Olay age-enhancing cream? Why, even after a hundred years, are you following in the same footsteps? Rather, why didn't you send her to find pepper spray? Or to a school where they teach kung-fu karate?'

Krishnadasi kept looking at her intently for a few moments. Then, suddenly, Krishnadasi, the older version of Rahdoi Ligiri, turned back and limped up to the reserved first coach in the metro train. Before the metallic door could close on her, Krishnadasi raised her hand in farewell and said, 'Hundreds of Rahdoi Ligiris travel in this reserved coach. They too carry a raw cut on their chest, cleverly hidden. There is no use sitting in the reserved Coach Number One in the metro. Search for a train in this world where you are considered first-class passengers.' The door of that hundred-year-old train closed.

She got up with a start in the middle of the night from that convoluted dream. A fragrant breeze washed the inside of her room, drowning the stink from the drain. 'Strange,' she murmured in her half-asleep, half-awakened stage, 'Do hasnahanas bloom even in this city?'

**Rahdoi Ligiri is a character from *Rahdoi Ligiri*, a novel written in Assamese by Rajanikanta Bordoloi in 1930 which depicts the tragic story of a beautiful maidservant Rahdoi in the royal palace in the late medieval period of Assam. She was raped and tortured to a point where she turned herself from an eighteen-year-old to an eighty-year-old through a secret yogic ritual and practice.

Kalindi, Your Black Waters . . .

Written the day after the night of Nirbhaya, this story is dedicated to all the raped and murdered women of the North-east and the world

Like a poet once said 'The desert that people abandoned for the garden. What remained were sulking, silent camels and traders who derived happiness from counting coins.'

Even deserts are green, along with the surreal crystal threads of moonlight and the mysterious blood-red flowers atop cacti.

Here, there is no moonlight, no flower, no music that emanates from the air passing through the leaves of a fruit-laden tree. Here, perched atop a concrete dome, there is a lonely tulsi plant that is breathing its last.

A number of sombre households surround that dying herb. The balcony of each house is secured with close-knit iron grills, giving the impression of a huge cage.

The afternoons are unique in this desert, which is made of rows and rows of cages for as far as one can see.

The intensely hot afternoons are further heated by dry, unrhythmic breathing—how self-centric.

This is a story from one such afternoon.

An auto van was moving along the narrow by-lane towards a house with a tiny barsati. Inside was a small folding bed, a folding table, a folding clothes hanger—a folding world.

Each item symbolized a makeshift, temporary life except for a huge tin trunk, which was filled with books—small and big volumes of fiction and non-fiction. The young woman, who was moving into the barsati as a tenant, carried a lot with her besides these material belongings.

A whistle that pierced through the deep patch of the segun woods, the collective scream of hundreds of cyclists as they pedalled through the long narrow road that bisected that never-ending green patch, the treasure-trove filled to the brim with heard, unheard and forgotten folk songs and a sacred hymn, a whirlpool of yellow butterflies. When thousands of yellow butterflies descended, similar to that incident in *One Hundred Years of Solitude*, she too had a surreal experience of getting lost in a whirlpool of yellow colour brought by those thousands fluttering wings. A half-sculpted, innocent, deaf deity sitting all alone on a hilltop, a group of people coming to see her off, and her father, mother, brother and sister's loving wishes, 'O *aijoni*, complete your studies and come back home safe.' The parting shot that repeatedly played in her conscience, '*Bhonti oye, aijoni oye.*' Dear sister, dear aijoni, my daughter.'

Here too some people called her dear sister, dear daughter, but with an intended twist.

Behen*** . . . madar**** . . . bhaad mein jao saali.
Behen**** . . . madar**** . . .
Madar**** . . . behen**** . . .

This was also a kind of goodbye—hurling abuses that painted an obscene picture of the private parts of a sister and a mother. The driver dumped her luggage and pulled away, rounding up the heated debate with a verbal arrow, '*Pata nahi, kaha kaha se chale ate hain,*' for not fulfilling his demand for more money. These verbal arrows had hit her repeatedly, aimed at her in different situations, different contexts, 'God knows where these people come from!'

How, when and where did they come from, over thousands of years of migration? Who came first?

Through the hills or the passes or the sea? Did they come on foot or on horseback or by ship? Who came, who went? Who overthrew whom to take control? Who got pushed over the boundary lines? Who knows? Who can tell?

Can history tell? Folklore? Who will question whom? God knows from where these migrating groups arrived. Didn't they have their own homes? Didn't they adapt to the local culture and become sons of the soil?

Who are the indigenous sons of the soil? Those who claim to be the true inhabitants of a place may have also arrived as migrants. During their migration, they would have displaced some indigenous tribes.

Migrants and indigenous people attack each other with verbal arrows of sarcasm and hatred. Each word oozes destructive fire: *Dakhar, Miyaan, Kooli, Pakis, Chinky.*

'Hey, Chinky! You have done everything on your own. I told you so many times, I will help you with the shifting . . . but no, you are Jhansi ki Rani reincarnate.'

As the vapours of the obscene words and heated argument conjured up a black cloud on her horizon, the phone call brought a ray of sunlight.

It was a call from the hero. She was fond of this hero. Their first meeting was quite filmy! A damsel in distress and a knight in shining armour.

It was Choti Holi, the day before Holi, the festival of colours. She was returning from the university when she was accosted by a group of youngsters. How simple children can be. How easily they speak their hearts minus the veneer of sophistication. How naturally and completely they adapt to the moral values and preaching of their peers and parents. Armed with *pitchkaris* filled with water, eggs, tomatoes and a bucket of thick, slimy blue-coloured water, they fell over each other to get to her, shouting, 'Wait, you Chinky. We will teach you a lesson.'

The hero made his entry at this moment. The heroine was saved. In exchange of a chewing gum, a friendship was established. The friendship which empowered him to clench his teeth and tease her in his artificial, guttural voice, 'Hey, Chinky', whenever he felt a tide of affection washing over him.

After the introductory conversation, she learnt that the hero was one of the brightest stars from another famous institution of higher education. Their non-stop telephonic discussions on history, culture, literature and philosophy soon graduated to his recitation of Amir Khusrau, Ghalib and Meer's couplets:

Woh is ittefaq se humse mile ki
Hum ajnabi bhi rahe aur mulakat bhi ho gayi
Usne itne nazakat se dil ko chuma
Ki roza bhi na tuta aur iftaar bhi ho gayi

In response to the voice that brought a beautiful fragrance into her life with his sensitivity of 'meeting of the two souls who remained strangers, like someone who had devoured the iftar delicacies without even breaking his fast,' she told him, 'Not Jhansi ki Rani man. Probably Maharani Gaidinliu. Or Brave Kanaklala. But you have never heard those names. I am Rongpharpi Rongbe—the slayer of the henchman who came to squeeze out milk from her breast for the pet tiger cubs of the atrocious king. Stop pulling my leg. I have work to do.'

There was plenty to do. The water connection in the bathroom was defunct, the tap in the kitchen sink was leaking and a few plug points were not working. There were sparks. Shit. She should have checked carefully when she came to look at the house. The main problem was the back door. The landlord must have had it freshly painted. A thick coat of paint was glued to the frame and, as a result, it would neither open nor shut.

Frustrated, she leaned against the wall, slid onto the floor, and dialled the number of the real estate agent who had got her the house. The dry voice from the other end replied, 'No worries, no problem. Everything will be taken care of. I have assistants to fix those problems. They will be there shortly.' Soon, a motorbike with three men came to a halt right in front of the building.

They got to work quickly. The temperature in the room shot up. With deft movements and an investigative gaze, they started examining the water pipes, the electric wires, the wooden planks and the iron locks. But they examined the inhabitant of the house with more curiosity, more intensity— her face, her hair, her curves. Fair, flawless skin—was it the colour of milk or butter? Her soft limbs like succulent tandoori chicken legs fresh out of the hearth. Her hair dark like the midnight when they returned home after smoking a joint or gambling. Slanting, half-open eyes, thin eyebrows.

One of the men whispered to the others, '*Dekh dekh, dekh is laundiya ko*. Look at her. It seems as if the creator didn't spend much time on her nose; he made do with a small chunk of flesh and hurriedly made two tiny holes.'

They absorbed each and every detail. Why were they so different? Their soft tongue that rolled so differently? How were they so different, the men wondered.

How were *they* so different, she thought. So different in their way of talking. Their tongue was rough, like the skin of a toad, and so was their behaviour. She got busy putting her belongings in their proper places and soon got lost in her thoughts. The hardships of life had made them rough, sapping the softness and sensitivity from their tongues.

Compared to the green hills of her native place, the land here was dry. The seasons here seem to wither with their endless wait for the monsoons. And there were those hundred years of war, invasions, the heartrending stories about the partition of the land and the subsequent hardships—weren't these reasons enough for hardening their tongue? She kept reasoning . . . may be that's why they had become like the sand of that desert. Like sharp swords, like mad tuskers in battlefields that destroyed without caring whom they were destroying. Like donkeys carrying heavier loads than their body weight or like camels deprived of water for hundreds of days.

Did they need water? The thought crossed her mind. She remembered what her father had said. He had told her about the beautiful custom of the inhabitants of the eastern hills. The custom of water posts.

Each village had water posts at entry points. They would make a bamboo platform and keep an earthen pitcher filled with water on it so that a passing traveller could quench his thirst and wash away the fatigue.

The three men, drenched in sweat, grabbed the glasses of water from the tray she held out to them. The first one whispered to the other two, 'She may look different, but she is a good soul. She has offered us water without even being asked. She realized we were thirsty. She is like my mother.'

The second one touched his moustache and said, 'That's the catch. Why is she offering water when we never asked for it? What does it mean?'

Gulping down the contents of the glass, the third one shook his head.

'It does not make sense. It may be a small gesture, but it carries some hidden message,' he commented with the air of a philosopher.

They took a small break and started pondering that hidden meaning.

Three men, three empty glasses!

Looking at them whispering, a memory of an incident from her native place crossed her mind. An incident involving three thirsty men who came into a house for a glass of water. Three army men!

One day, years ago, when armed revolutionaries had taken shelter from the army in the deep jungles, three soldiers entered a woman's house for a drink of water. They drank the nectar called water, the *sanjivani* for them at that moment. But another kind of beastly hunger overpowered them after they had quenched their thirst, and they started tearing the clothes off the body of the motherly woman who had just offered them water! It was a terrifying story, unheard of in her part of the hills. Her mind was once again filled with dark clouds, a feeling that stemmed from fright and pain, but one she couldn't fathom. But then she remembered the face of the kind-hearted colonel who had come to the village with a bag full of candies for the children and begged for forgiveness for the crime. 'The three will be punished beyond a court martial,' he had promised. She remembered the sweet taste of the candy that had melted in her mouth. Aah! There are enough good people in the world with hearts as soft as fluffy cotton balls, she thought and felt reassured. Like the old witch from her grandmother's bedtime stories, who pushed the dark clouds in the sky with her bamboo pole, she too tried to shake off the thoughts that clouded her mind. She picked up a song as her own bamboo pole, humming a sweet, peppy tone that never failed to lift her soul.

'Humming? Oh God, she is actually singing!' They were surprised as they stood still to listen to her. They did not understand the lyrics. 'What kind of a woman sings in front of three strangers? A lonely girl living among strangers? Why did she have to leave the security of her hometown and come all the way here?' they thought.

'Everybody is following the Western culture. Everything has changed, the nation, the time, the people. The women are trying to become men. There is no veil, no covering their modesty. Look at her, what is she wearing, revealing her white knees? A piece of cloth wrapped around like a short lungi? They walk around without any inhibition, they laugh out loud. They pair up with boys and dance in circles, they play music. Even their food habits are different. They eat everything—dog, cat, cockroach, snake, frog, tiger, fox. Yes, they eat everything.

'The men and women also drink alcohol together. Drinking homemade liquor, they dance around the fire through the night. They say they even dance carrying a human head. Don't they show in the movies, *jingalala, hum hum, jingalala*. Do you think these scenes come out of thin air? Had it not been true, they would never have shown it in films.

'These people know black magic. They turn people into lambs with their magic, sometimes into stone statues. Do you know?

'Everything is free and frank in their society. Men and women make out anywhere, anytime. No, it is not made up. It's completely true, and it is not as if such things happened long ago. That's how they live even today. There are still places where there are no roads, no cars, only thick jungle. These are uncivilized people. How strange, how repulsive, how dangerous.'

'What fun,' she thought as she kept humming the Chomangkan song. That Chomangkan festival, those groovy love songs and devotional songs in praise of the god Hemphu, which the entire community sang in unison with purity in their hearts, 'O Hemphu god, fill our fields with paddy, fill our minds with happiness.' In that spiritual note that fills up the body and soul, she got carried away, losing herself to that divine rhythm.

How can the same tune evoke two such opposite reactions in people? Why does the blood flowing in the veins of a perpetrator go berserk like that of a wild horse? Why do they create the divide between us and them? The men started losing themselves to animal instinct. 'She is not my sister, she is not my mother.' Without a prick on their conscience, they turned her body into a battleground.

Those who have just known relationships of two kinds—blood and fire—would never know that some relationships could be based on humanitarian grounds too. For those whom physicality is the only truth, how would they ever reach the level where the connecting thread between two people is nothing but sensitivity of soul and sensibility of mind? Those who are stuck with the misleading definition of their manhood, how will they ever be sensitive enough to recognize heart-to-heart bonding? For them manhood means forcing themselves onto a woman and breaking her into pieces. It is a competition—'look how big I am, with my erect tool, I can easily break this earthen toy—my wildness, my aggression is my manliness.' The other one contests him—'I can break this vessel with much more cruelty. Hence, I am more macho.' God alone knows whether they were caught up in some barbaric streak or the competition to prove their manhood, on the heartless afternoon they turned her body into a battleground.

All three, possessed with frenzy, turned into three battle horses, rampaging her fragile body. Who could break her more? The competition continued, stripping more and more flesh off her being. If one picked up a half-broken water pipe, the other one collected an electric wire, long enough to tie her limbs. The third one fished out a claw hammer meant to take out nails from a wooden plank. There was no pain, no conflict in their minds to stop them from doing what they were doing. She was not one of them. She was a strange creature from an alien place.

No pen has the strength to describe that terrible scene. No pen has the right to give the blow-by-blow details and consciously or unconsciously be part of some voyeuristic pleasure. No pen has the right to take that scene to a climax.

The pen can only look into the heart and ask, 'Why does it happen?'

Why does it happen, why did it happen? There will be many justifications. When this afternoon, drowning in a pool of blood, would finally turn into a dead evening and a dark spirited night, someone would say, 'This is nothing. Such things happen every day. What's new about it?'

Someone would blame it on that lonely afternoon, the soaring temperatures. Someone would blame it on Western culture and someone would blame it on the free primitive ways of that distant land. Someone would blame the dress code, someone the position of the stars in the sky. Someone would notice those three glasses. Not her flattened jawline, her bleeding lips, her broken fingers or her tied legs. They would only see those three empty glasses and raise the question: What did those three glasses contain?

Alcohol or drug-laced drinks? Collectively in a hushed voice, they would say, 'Maybe she asked for it, yes, she asked for it. Otherwise, why are there these three empty glasses? She must have offered them these glasses!'

While that afternoon was being choked with a dry pool of blood, the people were quietly inside their big cages. When the afternoon screamed with a muffled voice and a mute tongue in its numb lament asked, 'O mother, O father, why did you teach us to offer water even to strangers, why did you tell us about the water posts for unknown travellers?' Those people were enjoying their afternoon siesta after a hearty lunch. In that solitary world, only the silent chorus of a farewell snapshot was crying over and over again.

'Dear daughter, oye *aijoni*, come back home safe and sound.' As the dark clouds were slowly descending on that afternoon, the last hazy vision was dotted with a few familiar faces—of her mother, father, brother and sister, there was the face of a half-carved stone statue of a deity, a patch of segun trees, the sliding road of an undulating hill. Also, the faces of the people she saw during her visit to her uncle's place in the plains, making a dash to the poultry cage on the festive night of the Uruka.

As her life dragged itself to the door of death, halting, refusing to part with the tattered body, crying that it was not the time to go, the memory of that dreadful childhood night came flooding back. The faces of the hunters—her own neighbourhood boys who had come to steal ducks on that Bihu Uruka night. The abnormal glint in their eyes, their tightly drawn lips and their brutal laughter.

'Leave my ducks alone, leave them alone!' As she was about to scream, a gush of warm blood came out through the slit in her throat, where a piece of a broken water pipe had been shoved in. The red hibiscus of death fell on the floor.

* * *

Sitting on the mount of thousands of bloodstained hibiscus flowers was a thousand-year-old bird, Gidhraj, recording the scene in the frame of eternity. Having witnessed history since ancient times till that unfortunate afternoon, this mythical character sat on the tallest branch of the time tree in the folktale forest, from where he could watch the bloodstained afternoon.

This is the Gidhraj who lives on the blood of sinners, whom Krishna came to meet along with his friend Arjun, who was drunk with victory in the battle of Kurukshetra. Gidhraj looked at the proud Arjun and said sarcastically,

'The Mahabharata battle? What's so great about it? The bloodshed in that battle couldn't even wet the earth. I flew down to the earth to quench my thirst, but before I landed there, the soil had soaked up all the blood. The battle between Durga and Mahish was a true battle. Sitting on this branch itself, I could drink the blood that flew like a river. Who said Durga was a goddess with ten hands and the gods gave her their weapons to kill the demon Mahish? Durga had just two hands and fought with her own weapon but with what valour she fought! Mahish, who was not a demon but an amorous king gone wild like a buffalo bull in heat mounting every cow on sight, was cut into pieces with the piercing sickle of Durga on her way back from the paddy field. Blood flowed like a river for seven days and nights. Your battle of Kurukshetra, it couldn't even quench my thirst!'

Gidhraj remembered Arjun's ashen face as he left, his ego smashed into pieces. Perhaps Kurukshetra was not one of the greatest battles in the world, but what about that chapter associated with the battle? Has the world witnessed an incident so shameful ever again? Has it been recorded by any great poet in any other corner of the world? Shame, shame! A woman, dragged by her hair and stripped in the court of the king, in front of hundreds of honourable men in the court of justice.

Sitting on the tallest branch of the time tree, Gidhraj looked around. There she is, Kalindi Yamuna. Flowing in silence, the polluted and dying version of yesteryear's pure and cascading water body. That's Hasthinapur—the land of Indraprastha—the reason for the battle of Kurukshetra. It seems the repulsive chapter of stripping women naked has been the sole inheritance for the generations to come, be it from any *varna*, *jati* or *prakriti*. With helpless, tired eyes, Gidhraj looked at Kalindi Yamuna once again. He recalled the poet's tribute to Yamuna—the 'Yamunastakam'.

O, the one who has descended from the Mount Kalinda,
Kalindi you are the daughter of the sun,
You wash away the sins of the world,
And carrying those stains of sin,
Your water has turned black.

'Have you noticed, Kalindi,' Gidhraj called out, 'after washing the sins of all those sinners, you have become dark like the *Amabwashya* night.' Gidhraj's eyes grew moist. 'Did you see how that afternoon is lying lifeless amidst all the blood on your ghat? How another deadly hibiscus just bloomed on your shady bank? How frequently such hibiscuses are blooming from the pools of blood? Have you seen Kalindi, in Dhaula Kuan, Mahipalpur, Munirka, Vasant Kunj, everywhere, how the blood oozes out of so many uteruses, nurturing those hibiscuses? How huge the mound has grown? This bloodstream has surpassed even the one that rose from the Durga-Mahish fight. Look how this river of blood is about to wash out everything; it is reaching the tallest branch of this time tree. This tree will be submerged in the blood, but I will starve to death, Kalindi, as I drink only the blood of sinners, how can I drink the blood of the innocent?'

On the ghat of the silent, lifeless Kalindi, on the banks of the bloodstream, the thousand-year-old tired Gidhraj flapped his wings restlessly and hopped from one branch to another. He was thirsty to the soul. How long had it been since there was a fight between right and wrong, between justice and injustice? How long since he drank from the blood of the sinners to his heart's content? Everywhere there was only the blood of the innocent. The utter hopelessness and the thirst made his eyes blur. The thirsty Gidhraj, roaming aimlessly in the time-sky, saw, through his blurred eyes cast onto the future, the people emerging out of those rows of huge cage-like homes. People who otherwise kept to themselves in the safety of their homes, thinking it was someone else's neck which was on the line, were coming out in groups.

'How strange,' Gidhraj wondered, 'Have they finally realized that whether the eyes were slanted and small or big and well-defined, whether the complexion was fair or wheatish or dark, the teardrops were the same, warm and salty, the colour of the blood that oozed out of those mutilated uteruses was the same, hibiscus-red.'

Gidhraj was elated, bouncing with boundless joy he soared up into the sky, but couldn't help a sardonic smile on his face. 'Kalindi, look, finally they have come out to the streets in hundreds, finally they have realized that the fire has spread to their doorsteps. If nothing was done to douse it, that fire would engulf them too. The bloodstained hibiscus of death would bloom in their courtyard, in every courtyard.'

The Fireflies Outside of the Frame

In memory of Nido Tania, a young boy from Arunachal Pradesh who was killed in a mob attack in the streets of Delhi on 29 January 2014

That night the moon was not as pale as a fallen leaf. Neither did it resemble a skull as it did tonight. That moon was a different one. Shining bright amidst the twinkling stars, it belonged to a sky from his childhood. He was looking at it without blinking. At that point, another, more mesmerizing scene was unfolding before him—a strange procession in the dark corridor that started from the mankasu shrubs and spread up to the knees of the bamboos reaching to the sky. It was a congregation of hundreds of twinkling, flying lights, as if the stars had descended upon the earth and were standing in a queue to take off to a magical land. With spellbound eyes he kept looking at the thousands of fireflies that flew with their glowing tiny lanterns in that dark night.

Which scene was more enchanting, more incomprehensible? Unable to grasp this, his tiny soul was lost. For the first time in his life, he was waking up to the realization that under the surface of the familiar lay the entrance to an unknown reality. He had heard a stifled incoherent cadence, unfamiliar and unknowable. That unknowable something turned into the sound of a keteki bird. Bypassing that moon and the procession of the flying lights, the sound had entered his consciousness, luring him to an exotic land beyond time where a nameless pain embraced happiness.

'Come, come, haven't you finished yet? How long do you take to pee? Come, it's late. The world is fast asleep. Only the witches are awake, playing their tiny rattles. Come on, why are you standing still?'

He got a jolt hearing his grandmother's voice in close proximity. That night his grandmother had brought him back from the brink of an unknown territory to tuck him into her carved black mahogany bed. Putting her hands on his forehead she recited the *Dhyanityang Maheshang Rajatgirinibhang Charuchadraha* mantra and then followed the daily ritual of humming the song:

Pase trinoyan divya upavan
Dekhilata vidyaman
Phal phul dhari, jakmak kari
Ase jata brikhya mano

'What are you singing, grandma?'

'This is about the creation of the Almighty, son, the divine garden of heaven with innumerable celestial trees laden with nectar, flowers and fruits. What a beautiful composition, as if the Almighty Himself is the moon, his light of glory spreading everywhere.'

'What grandma, it's so boring. Why do you sing these songs every day, these hard slokas and songs that rhyme?

Why don't you ever sing Bihu songs? Don't you know any Bihu*geet*? Like Bogakai sings at the top of his voice while taking the cattle out to the field, while cleaning the cowshed, while tendering the gourd tendrils, "*Roya, roi roi roi boge paani khale goi.*"

'Now what is this *roya roi roi*—after waiting and waiting forever the egret finally drank the water! If my heart were a betel nut, I would have split it open to show you my pain. They're hilarious, these Bihu songs. Who cares if the egret drank the water or not? How can people be betel nuts?'

His grandmother grew quiet. In a barely audible voice, as if talking to herself, she said, 'I did not get an opportunity to hum Bihu songs, son. As soon as the Bihu songs started playing inside my heart, they put a tight leash on my lips and tongue. Bihugeet is not funny, dear. It comes out tearing one's heart, bathing in the blood, and reaches the lips. Pushing the pedals of the loom, gazing at the horizon in wait, when the eyes flow and the pitcher resting on the waist gets restless near the riverbank, then a person becomes soft like a raw betel nut which cannot be cut by a blunt knife.'

Falling asleep on some impenetrable bed of memories, a few scattered scenes came flooding back to his grandmother's eyes—a soft betel nut like a heart and a quiet afternoon.

An afternoon buried in the distant past; a meditative egret standing in the water under the blistering sun. There was another meditative figure under the huge tree close to the waterbody. It was a cowherd, his eyes forever searching for someone, like the egret in the water. It was in no hurry to quench its thirst. Far away, on the curve of the road, appeared a pitcher, set on a slender waist, filled to the brim with emotions. After an eternity of meditation, the egret drank water from the river. At that rare moment of ecstasy, pouring all his emotions into an expression of joy, a creative tune reverberated through the world, '*Roya roi roi roi, boge paani khale goi.*' The song of the cowherd collided with the pitcher, the water from the pitcher spilled over the carrier's bosom.

'We were not supposed to fetch water from the river. Going out with my friends to the bank was my undoing. In those days, son, upper-caste or upper-class women were not supposed to fetch water from the river. Nor were we allowed to sing Bihugeet. That day a Bihu song hit me like an arrow. I started humming it silently. Or had it sprouted inside me after the secret adventure to the river that afternoon? Needless to say, in those days, all the Bihu songs that would sprout in our dark innards were deprived of sunlight and air. They died a slow painful death within closed chambers.' With her inaudible voice his grandmother had made another confession in her silent soliloquy.

'Have you died grandma? Why have you gone so quiet? What are you thinking about, staring at nothing?'

A ray of light seeping in from the ventilator illuminated his grandmother's face. Hearing his voice, the iris of her eye danced back to life. He saw the moon hanging in between the iron rods of the ventilator.

* * *

The face of the moon resembled a skull. He was looking at it after so many years. He saw the pale face of the moon peeping through the window of the emergency ward, just above the ambulance parked outside. The red light of the ambulance switched on, followed by the wailing of the siren. The inert figure on the next bed got a jolt. He opened his eyes, which were covered with dried blood. His swollen nose, swollen cheeks and bandaged head made those eyes look like two small red pools sunken in dark crevices. With great difficulty he managed to ask him in Nagamese, 'Why are you still awake, Mita?'

'Mita'. . . Rizulu called him Mita! Rizulu reached out to him as Mita. Ah! He kept looking at Rizulu's eyes, and his swollen dark lips that had just uttered this word to him— Mita . . . It had taken years of bonding between two ethnic communities for this word 'Mita' to evolve. It had layers of meaning embedded in it. It was as sturdy and impermeable as the walls of the Talatal Ghar, the Rangpur Palace in Assam's Sivasagur, cemented with lentils and duck eggs. It was a word fortified with the emotions of a friend and a well-wisher. Leaning on that fort were his uncle and the father of the tattered body that lay in the emergency ward whose name was Rizulu. The word was a tree that germinated from a seed that came with the breeze blown from the hills of the Nagas and was nourished by the fertile soil of the plains of the Brahmaputra river. Breaking the barriers imposed by history with its rigid customs and traditions, rules and regulations and its stringent memories, the word branched out under a divine sky with all its glory. Some people took refuge under that sky, but their shelter appeared to be nothing but a transitory makeshift camp of thatched roof and frail bamboo on the ever-eroding bank of a river in rage. Though the unsparing truth of history had steadily destroyed the tent, that word, like a compulsive traveller, had now pitched a tent in this emergency ward. From the secure enclosure of the tent, two bloodshot eyes were looking at him. The bloodshot eyes of Rizulu, Rizulu Reo Angami, a boy from the hills of Nagaland.

'Rizulu Reo, right?' A policeman, stepping inside the emergency ward, volleyed him as soon as he turned his gaze away from the swollen tenderness of his bloodshot eyes to the bellowing at the door.

'You have not lodged an FIR, have you? He was unconscious when our patrolling van picked him up. How is he now? This is election time. Every party is on alert. It might be made into a campaign issue. It will make newspaper headlines. We are trying to speed up our investigations. Otherwise, there will be unnecessary politicization of the issue. We will get harassed. The blame game will start. Perhaps he can talk now. What about you? You tell us who you are and what you know.'

The policeman talked ceaselessly, 'You see, we are doing our duty even at this hour. There is no time to rest, not at all. Such incidents are only increasing by the day. Haven't you noticed? You people should be careful. Why do you roam around at night? Have you not seen how the people from your region are being targeted? Your girls, why don't they cover themselves up? If a deer comes and jumps enticingly in front of a tiger, the tiger will pounce. You people look different. You, of course, do look like one of us—many children of Ma Kamakhya and Baba Brahmaputra look like us—but some of you and those living in the hills and jungles look so different that it is difficult to imagine that they belong to this country. They look like they are from that other country, China. Look at him, he comes from your neighbouring land, who fought with us for a hundred years. They don't want to be part of this country, do they?'

The policeman was looking intently at his face, but the gaze couldn't reach his eyes which were roving around some faraway hills, in the lush green foothills, its crevices and cleavages where charred bodies lay hidden, burnt huts, burnt churches, burnt orange groves, the stench of those burnt lives was still alive like cockroaches flapping their dark brown wings amidst invasive clouds of thick radiation. Though the invasive platoons in camouflaged olive-green uniforms had disappeared, their shadows and the sounds of thunder-like guns still lingered on in those hills, in streams and wild berries, in lullabies and in the forgotten songs of nightmares. They no longer talked about these things; move on, move on, that's what we have always said, add soil and bury all, the wisest thing to do, whether it is heartbreak or the holocaust.

'You know, it seems nightmarish at times, the way we have to take pains cleaning the mess created by you people— you people behave so atrociously out here. You boys and girls openly hold hands, you eat anything and everything, your hairstyles are so exotic, like the Americans, there is no decency about the way you people dress. This is the capital of the country. You should know how to conduct yourself here!'

Startled, he came back from the hills to the hospital ward and heard the police official blabbering. Rizulu had shut his eyes a long time back. He was lying still like a dead body. Like Rizulu, the officer too was tired and tattered. Besides, he was sozzled. With his slurred tongue, he asked the doctor, who was on his last round of the night shift, 'Yes, doctor sahib, when can the patient give his statement?'

'Not a patient from some disease, officer. He is injured. The way the mob bashed him up, his bones are broken and there are internal injuries. It will take a couple of days to heal.'

'Such cases have been on the rise lately,' the policeman commented looking at the doctor. Giving him a smile, the doctor checked the saline bottle and replied, 'No, such incidents happened earlier too. These days the media is playing a proactive role in reporting them. These people feel confident to report them too. They are not the bad sort. I have been to that side of the country a couple of times. Good people. Affectionate, hospitable. We are only harbouring some misconceptions. Some of us have such weird perceptions, especially the older generation. We used to think they roam naked in the jungle, they eat cockroaches, lizards, even human beings, that they have not seen a school, college, phone booth, computer, TV, etc. There are no roads, nothing at all. Ridiculous. I am happy to see that the young generation nowadays is way ahead of us; they embrace all, they do not differentiate, they are open-hearted.'

'Maybe, but have you not seen where they live—in the areas around the city—how they huddle around the pharmacies and then sit like virus-infected chickens in those shady by-lanes? After sniffing, puffing or injecting, how their inert bodies lie slumped there? Their red apple-like cheeks turn rotten—the addicts, they look like ghosts.'

'Where do you not see such ghosts, dear sir?' thought the doctor. He had no intention of starting an argument at this hour in the emergency ward. He pondered again, 'These ghostly figures roam about everywhere. Otherwise, how did the rows of trucks from across the border, smuggling piles of white powder packets and Afghan hashish, enter the country without getting caught? How did thousands of purple plantations bloom miles after miles in this part of the country too, north and upward of this capital? You are aware of it, sir, this is old history spreading across several centuries. Why do we always point fingers only at a select few, criminalize only a certain section?'

However, after going through a hell of a draining day with a dog-tired soul and body, he did not feel like arguing. The SHO and his assistant's tongues, too, were slowly getting tied into knots due to alcohol and exhaustion. He could only quietly announce, 'Sir, don't worry, you are not the only one to fall into this trap of typecasting humans on the basis of their looks, skin, colour, caste, creed, religion and location. Everyone falls into this trap, sir.'

Yes, everyone fell into this trap. Friends of Rizulu Reo's father used to call him a dog-eater. Patronized by a missionary father, Rizulu's father had come down from the Naga hills to the plains of the Brahmaputra to study in the government school in the district headquarters. Rizulu's Mita had heard this from his uncle, who was a classmate of Rizulu's father. How his classmates from the plains would catcall whenever they had a spat, 'Dog-eater, dog-eater!' Vikeshoo Reo, the dog-eater who roams naked in the hills.

He had heard another hair-raising story as well.

During a summer vacation, his uncle had invited Rizulu's father for lunch. His great-grandmother served Rizulu's father lunch on a banana leaf and made him sit on the veranda of the loom shed near the cowshed. Whereas his uncle had placed a wooden stool for his friend on their kitchen floor. Alarmed, his uncle asked, 'Grandma, why are you serving Vikeshoo his food outside? Why on a banana leaf instead of a bell metal plate?'

'They are *melesh*, untouchable, lower caste people, son. They cannot enter our kitchen.'

God alone knows what possessed his uncle as he screamed at his grandmother, 'Why did you not get buried along with the goat in that big earthquake, you old witch?'

Seeing his uncle, a schoolgoing child, revolting against his parents for the sake of his friendship with Vikeshoo, a Naga from the hills, his grandfather, angry as hell, pulled out the burnt wood from the hearth and beat him black and blue. Scared, the young boy wet his pants. Long black lines covered his entire body. Bearing testimony to the incident was a long black cut on his forehead. Similar to his uncle's scar, Rizulu's father too had one on his mind for the rest of his life.

'Will these scars ever go away,' he asked the nurse who was applying some ointment on the cuts on Rizulu's face and chest. The police officer and the doctor had just left the room. Since the night before, curious, tense footsteps were continuously walking in and out of the emergency ward. So many people, so many questions! Various groups of people were coming and going—overzealous journalists from newspapers and television channels, human rights activists, citizen's security forum members, people from various political parties, student union leaders from the hills and plains of the seven sisters. With great difficulty, Rizulu could narrate the incident to one reporter. How around 9 p.m., after leaving the metro station, he was walking home. How he was accosted by a group in the dark corner of a park. How they shouted, 'Hit him, hit him—finish the Chinky today.'

Though he narrated the incident, he refrained from mentioning that among those who had closed in on him like he was Abhimanyu in the *Chakravyuh* were a few familiar faces. He saw them every day in the neighbourhood. He was beginning to grow fond of them. A few days ago, he had heard that they had organized a secret meeting with the landlords of the houses who rented out their small *jhuggis* and barsatis. A secret meeting of the panchayat. 'The house owners have formed a unique panchayat,' Yengtham Boycha had whispered inaudibly in a tense voice over a bottle of rum, and plates of pork fry and dry fish. 'You have these gully panchayats in the very heart of the national capital! Just a little distance away from the Supreme Court and Parliament House.' The panchayat had decided to evict those like him from that area. For a couple of days, the whispers made the air thick with tension. After a few days, some government officials and NGO workers were seen. They were mediators. Some kind-hearted, sympathetic people had warned them—just be careful.

Be careful of his own people in his own country? Rizulu had felt like laughing; in his veins surged the blood of his grandfather, Kotcha Reo Angami. Why should he be afraid? That day he took out the last memorabilia of his grandfather, a dog tag, and kept fiddling with it. The shiny bronze dog tag had once adorned his grandfather's chest. Why did you not tell that journalist about your grandfather, Mita?

They too had carried forward the tradition of the word Mita. Initially, of course, just for fun. Later, the word had tied them together. In a firm knot like the one that binds two bamboo poles in a pyre cot. Companions even in death.

'Why did you not tell them how your grandfather died? Let them all know—everyone should know—the boy they bashed up in the dark alley and left half dead just because they thought he was not from this country, not one of them, is actually Azad Hind Fauj's General Kotcha Reo's bloodline. I have heard the tale of your grandfather, that brave young man from Khonoma village! That young man had left along with Fizo to enrol in Subhash Chandra Bose's revolutionary army, Azad Hind Fauj. Marching with the Japanese army, they came forward from Jesami to Kohima, travelling through hostile terrain, carrying the heavy weight of guns and dead buffaloes and pigs on their shoulders. They had nothing to eat but a buffalo leg one day, the other leg the next day. The jawans filled their tummies with just a little meat. There were no tents to sleep in. Tying a cloth from one branch to another like a hammock, they had spent the nights looking at the open sky and later dreamt of an independent nation where everyone would be free and equal. After walking a thousand miles through the thick, dark forest, climbing serpentine trails in the undulating hills day after day, losing count of passing time, their swollen legs looked like elephant leeches. But those legs did not stop walking towards that dream. Two of those legs were Kotcha Reo Angami's and his neck, like other jawans, was adorned with a metallic pendant—the Azad Hind Fauj's secret sign, the dog tag. Your grandfather's dog tag is a rare symbol, a priceless collection from our history's archive. Why didn't you tell the journalist about that? You didn't even tell him that you knew those people who attacked you. Why? Will you tell the people about this rare dog tag or not? Let's do a feature on it in the Sunday Special of *The Hindu*. Let's call the journalist.'

'I won't tell them. I won't. Why should I? What would happen even if I tell them?'

Rizulu seemed upset. One could see a deep cynical curve at the corner of his lip. Rizulu had closed his eyes, but his friend knew he was awake. He also knew what Rizulu was thinking. He could read his Mita's mind vividly—did anyone really care? Had anyone so far remembered anything with an unselfish motive? Things had been erased deliberately, pages of history forgotten. Only the chapter of dissent was chanted like a mantra whenever a memoir of our land was written. Was there a history book that told the entire truth? In some footnote or in the reference section? In the prologue or in the epilogue? Had anyone ever even scribbled a note in the margin with a pencil dedicating a few sentences to their history, their narratives?

With emotions swelling up like a raincloud, he looked at Rizulu's face, expressionless, like a detached Buddhist monk. Only a nameless expression made his eyelids quiver, and he opened his eyes suddenly. Looking at him, Rizulu said, 'You know what? I am tired. We have been fighting since the day we were born. In fact we have been fighting since before our birth. Carrying the baggage of bloodline—caste, community, race, religion—we have just been fighting with one another. We are the gunslingers with barrels of rotten prejudices. All this fighting has made me tired. Very tired. I am tired as a human being. Tell me, why do I have to tell them Kotcha Reo Angami's story? Why do I have to beg for my life, citing my history—listen, O' nation, I too am your child. I am not an illegitimate child. I am not a bastard. I too am your son. Don't beat me. Don't break my fingers. Don't bang my head. Brothers, I too can sing the national anthem. My forefathers had sung that song while marching from Jesami to Kohima with their rifles and carrying dead buffaloes on their shoulders day and night. They had sung a song in their own tongue too. Some wanted to sing only that song, their own song and nothing else, and they had fought like mad panthers for that, but at times they had sung this song too—this anthem.

'This is not the main thing. The main thing is, why? Why can't I, just like anybody else, walk at night without fear? Do I not have that right—as a human being under this sky? That's why I am tired, Mita. This visage, these slanting eyes, this spiky hair and this yellow skin—I have no control over these attributes. Nor did I have control over my inherited history and customs. These are integral to me—will remain so till my death—but my mind, my soul sometimes asks me—can I not throw all these away and be naked? Like a prehistoric man, can I not become a citizen of this earth? Can I not return home without fear after watching a late-night movie? Why do I need another dog tag around my neck?'

Rizulu started panting. One by one, he was shedding the baggage of a lifetime that had been weighing him down. He had never seen Rizulu talk this much. As he talked and panted, a stream of blood flowed out of the corner of his mouth. The nurse who came running from the emergency wing scolded him with a stern caution, '*Oi pagla gaya hain kyaa*—man, have you gone mad.' She made him drink some antibiotic-laced water. 'Your friend will sleep for hours.'

Rizulu went into a deep sleep, but he was not sleepy. Standing by the window he saw the pale yellow dying moon in the sky. The moon which looked like a fallen leaf, like a skull. The moon no longer looked like the moon of his childhood hanging on to the ventilator; this was a different moon.

The moonlight had fallen on his grandmother's face. Her body was still, her eyes were focused on something far away. 'Have you died grandma, have you died grandma, grandma?' Returning to that silent night of his childhood, he pushed his grandma once again, 'Grandma, O' grandma, have you died?'

'No, son, what happened? Do you want to ask something? You are not sleeping?' He saw the moon hanging from the iron railing of the ventilator. In the southern corner of the mosquito net, there was a firefly twinkling. The scene he had witnessed when he went to the hijol tree to answer nature's call had come back to him. He had asked his grandmother, 'Tell me, grandma, which is more beautiful—which is bigger—the moon or the procession of the fireflies?'

'Each one is big and beautiful in its own place, little one! Each one has its own significance and uniqueness. Each truth has its own light. Everyone has their own truth. The divine truth of the heavenly garden of the Almighty is the same as the earthly truth of the egret in the Bihu song or a raw betel nut. You know what, son, the moon shines from borrowed light but the fireflies glow in their own light that emanates from their inner luminescence.'

After so many years, standing by this window, he finally understood the meaning of his grandmother's words. He gazed back at Rizulu's face. Wrapped in bandages, his face looked white, icy white, the colour of death. In an inaudible whisper he called out to his friend in silence, 'Brother, Mita, I can understand the reason for your tiredness. Like you, I too feel tired at times. But you know what, looking at this pale skeletal moon from this hospital ward and standing near you now, I recall a forgotten scene, which had lit the dark corridor of a childhood night with the twinkles of a hundred fireflies and created an empire of radiance, and I recall Grandma's wise words.'

He came back to sit on the plastic chair near the bed. He wished he had a piece of paper. He took out the prescription from his pocket and started scribbling on the back. From this high window frame, one could just see the moon, not those fireflies flying in the fringe. Yet, how many such firefly processions were around, flying on the unseen periphery! 'Isn't it time to talk about those fireflies, to write about their light? It's the turn of the fireflies now, the faraway fireflies outside this frame.'

Mayur Vihar

For those who still believe in love . . .

Perhaps I had really heard it. Or imagined it? I did hear it. Just once. Just outside the window. Slicing through the shell of the night, it came out of its deep womb, and the throaty sound made the air vibrate. What a rude, screeching pitch, originated from the high octane of musical notes. Though I had heard it for the first time, I was sure that it was the sound.

Early in the morning, in a voice trembling with excitement, I told my father, 'Last night I heard the sound of a peacock, father.' Father was sitting on the dhurrie in the puja room, with the oblong copper vessel filled with water and the bell metal plate containing blades of grass and milky white durun flowers in front of him. In the morning, when the fog and sun played hide and seek over an area which bore no evidence of a peacock living within miles, my father received this piece of news quietly and stared at me. Giving me his usual poignant smile, he said, 'Really? How nice. You are indeed lucky. They must be around. In the deep jungle and hills, there must be a peacock, hiding away from us, dancing around with its open feathers. Do you know, according to the *Jatakas*, Gautam Buddha, in one of his early incarnations, was born as a peacock. A golden peacock.'

Like he did every day, he started teasing me by reciting his self-composed couplet: 'Come one day, friend, will I be lucky enough to hear your melodious voice in the midnight, will I be lucky enough to see your blue face—how do I express my pain, my heart breaks when I don't get to see your moon-like face. Will I ever get to see your moon-like face at midnight?'

After completing his recitation, he picked up the water vessel and the puja thali, and walked towards the courtyard, but stopped for a second to talk to himself, 'Anything surreal we get to hear, we hear only at midnight. Anything incomprehensible that happens, happens only at midnight. At the junction of subconscious and unconscious, dream and illusion, we stand face to face with them.'

Certain incomprehensible incidents do take place in the daylight too. Like what had happened the previous day, prior to the night when I had heard the peacock. It was between ease and uneasiness. Class seven is when childhood dignity was giving way to a hint of adolescent fancy. The time to make a desperate attempt to hide the two fast-developing conch-flower buds by gathering the white shirt in the front, above the long blue skirt. Two plaits neatly tied with red ribbons culminating in flowers managed to shield those buds. Droplets of sweat that had accumulated on the forehead were tickling the black bindi between the brows, the bindi we had made by rubbing the flat end of a big nail on the cooking pan to blacken it by the smoke from the

earthen hearth and oil. Decked up with the bindi and two
neat braids, as I was walking across the playfield towards
the tube well to drink water during recess, the air buzzed
with thousands of black bumble bugs. God alone knows
where the bumble bugs like black clouds came from and
covered the entire sky. Looking up, I saw him. The tall, lanky
boy who had come from the lower Assam area and joined
Class 12 at our school. The time after had neither a beginning
nor an ending. The buzzing sound of those black bugs was
fast turning into a thunderous noise. He grabbed my hand
tightly. In his solid grip, my fingers looked like a closed night
queen flower. In a sudden move, he inserted a long needle-like
thorn from a hiju tree into one of my fingertips.

'What are you doing, hey, why are you doing this . . .
what's this?' The question did not leave my lips. I was silently
trembling. The question came like an arrow from our English
teacher's lips. He was like a fresh whiff of breeze from the
river. Intelligent and sensitive, he was a young man who, after
completing his graduation from the most famous college in
the state, had come to replace Ajaya *baideo* for three months.
After childbirth, baideo would be back and sir would go away
for further studies in the national capital. Sir was different.
After classes, he would take us on a wandering and wondrous
trip of history, culture and philosophy. He loved poetry. From
him we heard, for the first time, about Lorca, Neruda and
Ghalib. Our day is a green apple cut into two, he would
recite. We learnt how Van Gogh had chopped off his ear and,
holding that bloody ear, had run into an obscure dark dismal
room of a brothel.

His face wore the look of a dark, dingy brothel room.
'Why did you do such a heinous thing? I won't punish you.

I won't even tell anyone, but you tell me honestly, why did you prick her finger with that hiju thorn? Why didn't you give her a hiju flower instead?'

Listening to Sir, the boy's eyes welled with tears. He looked at me and then at Sir, and fished out a green guava from his pocket. 'I had actually called her to give her this. I don't know what happened to me.'

I looked at the guava. It was a strange fruit. The outside was raw green. Inside, bright pink like a godhuligopal flower. Looking at the outside, it was difficult to imagine that the inside would be so ripe and pink. He said his uncle had a baby parrot for a pet. Whenever he looked at it, he felt like caressing its head and chest, but as soon as he held it in his hands, his heart would do somersaults, he would feel like twisting its neck and chewing it alive. She reminded him of that baby parrot.

The baby parrot simile had not been spoken of in front of Sir or me. Many years later, on one of the night outs with whiskey and charas, tossing and turning in a whirlpool of nostalgia, he had vomited out the whole episode to his close friends.

Tossing the guava, he kept looking down with teary eyes. Sir started murmuring a poem. Christopher Marlowe: 'Was this the face that launch'd a thousand ships, and burnt the topless towers of Illium? Sweet Helen, make me immortal with a kiss . . .'

Though I couldn't make head or tail of what the poem was suggesting, the words gave me goosebumps and looking at his palms, I thought, 'In one of his hands there is this delicious green-pink guava and in the other, there is a sharp thorn. How paradoxical.'

A paradox existed even in the moon-faced poem of father's composition. In one hand, a flute, in the other, a chakra. Didn't he, the one who created a mellifluous stream with his flute, use the same fingers to move the Sudarshanchakra and create a cascading stream of blood? The battle of Kurukshetra was visible to all. The bloody Kurukshetra he created in innumerable hearts remained invisible forever. The bugle of such an invisible Kurukshetra sounded in my heart that afternoon, and that night I heard the sound of the peacock.

I had heard its sound, but I was dying to see it before my eyes. The burning desire to be consumed by thousands of blue eyes remained glued to my being like a tick stuck to the skin. Its unseen wild, passionate dance in the evening had my pulse racing. Even if I didn't see it, I must find a fallen feather.

I found it. Years later. Years ago. During the month-long trip to the South from the department of art history. Our student group had been roaming the ruins of the Chola-Chalukya kingdoms. What an unusual and wonderful terrain it was. An undulating topography spread across miles. Perhaps the rock beds had given the topography its undulating nature. I don't remember whether it was the remains of the Chalukyas' kingdom or the Cholas', but I remember clearly that covering that huge rocky terrain was this olive-green moss kingdom. I remember those ruins of various kingdoms, bearing the testimony of how insignificant and transitory human life is. That day the moon, which made its appearance just when the sun was about to set, resembled a bone from a human skeleton. Trying to find my foothold in the skeletal moonlight, I lost my way. The road to the camp was gobbled up by the mossy empire and, along with it, all my companions. I went cold like a reptile. What to do, where to go? I saw from far, a light, making circles in that undulating terrain, fast approaching me, until it fell on my face. It was a torchlight.

The torch-wallah said, 'I knew for sure that you would get lost.' When we were about a yard from the campsite, he switched off the torch and in that mysterious dim moonlight, he looked at me and smiled. The white teeth on that dark face dazzled.

Before this, the torch-wallah had smiled his dazzling smile twice. The first time in the morning, when I was sitting in front of my camp as I had forgotten to pack my toothbrush. Breaking a small twig from the neem tree near the campsite, he had offered it to me, saying, 'I knew you would forget to pack your toothbrush,' and another time, when I was washing dried mud off my feet after I had slipped on a muddy patch. He had brought me a bucket of water, smiled and said, 'I knew you would slip in that mud.' That torch-wallah was our companion for just one month. He was the driver of the bus we had hired for the excursion. On one of the days during that unforgettable journey, I finally found a peacock feather in the rocky ruins. The white stem of the feather was a long one.

Sometimes, like the long white stem of the peacock feather, a few moments also seemed drawn out. As if they would never end. They would flow into eternity. Moments of waiting. Days spent in the waiting room of the railway station. Evenings waiting to hear that desired knock at the door. Wanting to see, looking around to hear, life constantly going around in circles in search of something . . . it seemed all too long at times. Hearing the harsh sound, without admitting that it was harsh, picking up that discarded bright piece of evidence from the ground, the desire to look at the complete entity becomes an eternally unfulfilled route. The way it had become for my father. That pining in his composition for the moon-faced blue cowherd boy from Brindavan. 'What do I talk about my pain, my heart breaks when I don't get to see your moon-like face.'

My father left the world without seeing that moon-like face. Perhaps he did. In a flash. Like I did. One moon-like face or the other. The silhouette of a peacock feather visible for a moment in the light radiated from the moon-like face. Sometimes pushing my way out of the crowd at the central metro station as some familiar strangers pass by, and one of them sniffs at the torn pages of a dog-eared book and closes his eyes. Sometimes walking along the pavement, one runs into a mob about to bash up a teenaged pickpocket and someone spreads his arms to shield him from the maddening crowd, like Govardhan protecting the residents of the Braj against Indra's destructive shower and lightning with a huge Govardhan umbrella. In these promising moments, in the reflection of a police van or in the translucent light of the pale moon, the moon-face appears in a flash and disappears just as quickly.

In the thick envelope of fog, the familiar route of my walk had disappeared that morning, long after that excursion in the ruins of the ancient kingdoms with the torch-wallah. I had settled in another kingdom, the kingdom where the past walks hand in hand with the present. The brick walls of the Purana Qila scoff at the new steel flyovers, old graveyards and *maqbaras* reluctantly put up with new shopping malls and multiplexes. The old mocks the new, the new rejects the old. However, during the ice-cold winter, they all surrender to a cruel king named fog who comes to reign, and everything becomes invisible.

Nothing was visible beyond a few feet that winter morning. I walked ahead, crossing the flyover and the sleepy silhouettes of rows and rows of high-rise apartments. The construction work for another highway had just started. The makeshift tents of the construction labourers were submerged in the fog, a completely silent, serene world. Bypassing a quiet lane, as I paused to catch my breath, I heard somewhere close by, somewhere close to the road, the sound of someone panting heavily and blended with that were moans and groans and some incomprehensible muttering. Moving a few steps closer to the source, I saw, amidst the stone-sand-iron domes, a still figure lying on the ground and riding it was another figure, like a possessed soldier riding a horse. Engrossed, he was fast climbing another peak. Seeing me, he fell from that peak of desire and neighing like a horse, he ran into the obscurity of the fog. Getting closer, I saw an unconscious, injured woman. Blood from the corner of her mouth had started to clot. Her sari, hiked up to her navel, was smeared with dust. From the tummy to the area between the thighs, there was a raw gash, covered with blood and pus. I shouted at the top of my voice, calling for help, and a few people came running from the labourers' tents. People with their migrant dreams of finding a home with a roof. One of the women said, '*Arey*, she is the woman from tent number seven. She gave birth to a child only a month back. Before that she was injured while working. How come she is lying here? Did she get drunk last night? Or pass out because of a stomach ache? Did a car hit her? She must have been lying here all night. *Ya* Allah, the devil cast his eyes on her.'

The devil had cast his eyes, indeed. The devil that had disappeared into the fog. Suppressing the urge to puke at the repulsive realization that the devil's desire hadn't even spared an unconscious, injured body, I saw, despite that thick fog, the huge nameplate on the massive metal pillars of the metro station shining—Mayur Vihar.

Mayur Vihar. There was no evidence of any *mayur*, any peacock, within miles and miles of this metropolitan vista which boasted of row after row of tall buildings and flyovers. There was the skyscraper of Hotel Hilton. On the other side there was the heavily congested industrial hub. Flowing in front, carrying all the industrial waste, was the stinking tar-like stream called *ganda naala*. Who named it Mayur Vihar? Had anyone seen a roving peacock's dance in this anarchy?

'Have you seen it, Lokesh? Have you ever seen it?' While visiting my artist friend Lokesh's house for dinner a few days later, I noticed a painting in his living room. There was a silhouette of a man in the frame and a peacock sleeping on his lap, like the bird I had been looking for. A vibrant golden hue and intricate designs on those long purplish-blue feathers. How beautiful, how desirable. 'Where did you see this? Where did you spot it? This golden peacock? How did you paint this?'

'No yaar, I have not seen it. Not till date. I might have heard its voice. Sometimes I pick up a feather, sometimes I see the mythical form for a second, on a canvas or old palm leaf, hear it in a Yiddish folk song or a Jataka tale. Maybe I saw it in a dream, heard the voice in some midnight maze of desire, how does it matter anyway yaar, just have faith in it.' Lokesh garbled, guzzling another extra-large peg.

I looked at Lokesh's painting for a long time. The silhouette of the man somehow started resembling my father and I heard my father's baritone, 'It exists. Somewhere in the by-lanes of this city, in the drains and sewers, in the smog and the fog, amidst the jungle of pipes and hills of plastic, it roams silently. It is there, it is there. It must be living somewhere, otherwise why on earth did we decide to call this dry harsh concrete jungle Mayur Vihar?'

The Final Leap of the Salmon

Dedicated to the surrendered rebels of the United Liberation Front of Assam (ULFA) who returned to engage in social welfare work for the state and the country

Prologue

Dear visitor of the night,

That night, leaning on the railing of the veranda, you narrated a beautiful story. You said that every narrator is a wordsmith or wordisan. Listening to you, I remembered Kabir Das and his *doha, 'Chadaria jhini re jhini'*. He was a volcano of words, one who wove chaddars of multiple threads on his loom and hundreds of *chadarias* of verse with his words. Looking at the pitch-black sky, you complained, 'Why had I not woven such a chaddar with my words? So many people have woven Vrindavani *vastras* with black and white strings of powerful words, but I am only a poor narrator. The way the poet had said, "My voice is feebler than the sound of a cricket," I had my doubts that I would ever be able to successfully map either the size or the intensity of your larger-than-life dream.'

Like those words, dreams too are carved. Each has its own colour, shape and texture. Even a single word, a single dream comes with many different images and potential, just the way the ordinary sunrise becomes the potent source of light and energy or turns into millions of radiating atoms in the unfolding spectacle of the universe. If a single word has so many different shades, then what about a dream? Especially if that dream is a collective one. Words cannot be strung together without giving them a thought. Collective dreams cannot just be interpreted. Some dialogues, some comparisons, some examples cannot be comprehended without experiencing them. To even attempt to reconstruct them with long narratives based on the imagination would be nothing but arrogance. However, heeding your advice, I took up the challenge. I liked your allegory. Keeping it as a reference point, I put up my torn, entangled threads of words into the word-loom to spin a *bihuwan* as a tribute to those brief moments you spent with me on the veranda. You probably remember that day—the nuni tree was in full bloom in the bright brown colour of abundance. Wherever you may be, whatever condition you may be in, climbing a steep path step by step, lying on a stressful bed or blowing smoke rings, my murmurs will find you. There remains a layer of cynicism at the core of my heart to put my faith in God, but I sincerely wish the tiny angels in Raphael's paintings descend on your horizon—those who flap their golden wings around Mother Mary or Madonna.

I

The sleuth was waiting at the mouth of the waterfall. It was falling with all its might and looked like a pure white flannel chaddar of hundreds of watery threads. The eyes of the bears were fixed on the chaddar hung on an invisible clothesline. The eyes gleamed like that of a hunter. Looking at their eyes intently was a shoal of salmon. The shoal looked like intense, swollen, restless waves, diving into the air, and crashing into billions of tiny liquid balls. Having travelled across many nautical miles, it had stopped there, and looked up for a glimpse of the mouth of the waterfall.

Above, a clear blue sky. Below, a grey rippling water table. In between, hanging in the air, a watery flannel chaddar. On one side of that chaddar stood the gang of predatory bears, their mouth salivating in anticipation, hunching down to catch the salmon. And on the other side, nearing the last leg of their life cycle, the shoal, swimming against the current, coming back to its place of origin, eager to cross the deathtrap laid by the predatory bears and the tall hurdle of the cascading waterfall. Looking up at the sky in unison, the salmons seemed to be saying a silent prayer, as if before their final leap against the giant wave, they were pleading to the Almighty, 'If we fall into the bear's mouth or die crashing on the rocky surface, O divine power, take us to our place of birth. There is no question of depriving our thirsty souls any longer.' Immediately after this, forming a huge wave, they created a scene that made one's heart stop. Moving against the current, in their bid to jump over the fall, they made the leap. The chorus of thousands of ascending salmons reverberated in the sky, making a strange sound—salaat!

With that sound his heart leapt out of his chest. After so long. Till then his heart had been beating feebly, like that of a fish lying on the dry sand of a riverbank. Since his return from the treacherous hills and deep jungles, his heart had been struggling like the fish gasping for air or the flickering wick of an earthen diya. He had been bedridden.

His body was not dying, his soul was. With a comatose soul, he lay on the bed, listening to the faint beating of his dying heart. The smoke released through his nostrils created a hazy screen as if the room was dying as well. The only thing alive was the vibrant rectangle—the television screen that cut through the silence. The strange animals on the Animal Planet channel mocked him—'Get up, get up, how long do you want to sleep, you bipedal animal? Look at us, man, learn a thing or two, open that door and venture out into the world.'

His heart was immovable, but the moment the shoal of salmon made that cyclonic leap against the current, it hit his almost-dead soul with all its force and threw him into a pool of rejuvenating water. How strange are salmons! After birth, they travel enthusiastically downstream to enjoy their youth, and, having spent a major part of their lives exploring the seas, they ultimately return to their place of birth, braving the strong upstream current. Overcoming many a hurdle in the process, they return for procreation and death. The mystery of travelling downstream and then coming back against the waves hung heavy on his senses. Unable to bear that heaviness, he closed his eyes. The light from the television set, the only source of light in that room, had blinded him.

They say one should not lie in a dark room at twilight. This was the time when the asura king Hiranyakashipu was done to death. He recalled the story from the Puranas his mother had told him when he was a child. His mother, whom he had seen after two decades, had become waif-like. With a figure as light as feathery cotton, the persona of his mother had become incomprehensible, like a fragile, weightless and airy source of light.

His brother's knife-like tongue was enough to bring him back from the surreal world. Attacking him with that knife, he asked, 'Why has a woman who used to be like a full moon slowly wasted away into a crescent moon? Look at the woman who deteriorated every single day after you left. Now that you are back, she is busy cooking all sorts of delicacies. This species called the mother is spineless. For their offspring or anybody under their care, they become spineless like the earthworm. You use them as bait in your selfish fishing rod or insensitively step over them—it does not matter. Their affection for their children will always remain fertile. All women in love—how they turn into spineless creatures.'

Twisting his knife in slow motion, which he did to impart a lesson on reality, he would often thunder on like a silencer-less motorbike. Slicing his conscience open, his brother often sprinkled the salt of intense revulsion and hatred on his wounds. It seemed like rhythmic stanzas of a hate song. Indeed, rolling out of a Black Dog, single malt-lashed tongue, it was a parody of a song that was part of their childhood games.

They used to play a game called 'hoppity hop butterfly'. The main player would call out the name of something and the others would go hunting for it. For example, 'Hoppity hop butterfly, where have you seen a kadam tree?' Slowly the game would get complex. 'Hoppity hop butterfly, where have you seen a four-legged bearded oldie?' Someone would point at the goat far away and jump with glee. Sometimes the game would become a complex puzzle.

Twelve villages with a beautiful story,
Each village has five houses,
In the village live two brothers,
They live hand to mouth, day in and out,
Hoppity hop butterfly, where did you see such a
phenomenon?

Someone would point at his father's wristwatch.

With a slurry tongue, his brother would sing that childhood song while clinking his tall glass

The one who survived on drink and corn,
The one with tick-laden skin and bloody hands,
The one who survived disease and diarrhoea,
The one who survived the bullets of the Burmese and the
Indian Army,
The one who entered the jungle like a tiger and came out
like an owl,
Even after return, who is living like a dead stinking fish,
Hoppity hop butterfly, where have you seen such a
strange being?

He would never get provoked by his brother's parody. Rather, he felt affectionate towards him. Sometimes love, too, made the tongue razor sharp. The parody from those childhood days comforted him. The cuts from the razor-sharp knife were never permanent. They just scratched the surface. The marks would eventually evaporate like naphthalene balls.

What remained was just an abstract narration in the form of a dream. Creating ripples in the still, colourless water of time. That dream would swim upstream and throw him mercilessly at the sands of dilemma and regret, like the salmon scattered on the other end of the waterfall. Jumping against the waves, the shoal had already crossed over the waterfall, ready to resume its journey to the place of its birth.

A few of them had landed in the mouth of the predatory bears.

He felt scared. Ever since he had come back, he was scared all the time. What if he, too, had ended up inside the mouth of a bear? Those were the bears of temptation. They were waiting to devour him like they did so many others. Like the salmons, his journey, too, was jinxed. An uncertain journey on an unknown path, guided only by a dream and the universal desire for liberation. If a journey had to end up in the mouth of a bear, what was the meaning of all this? Fearful, he coiled up like a millipede. With a coiled-up soul, he asked himself, 'Why did I embark upon that journey? Why did I leave everything to climb those hills? To join those groups hiding and camping beyond those hills and their deep jungles to give shape to their dreams of liberty?'

'What made you take the decision to form a united liberation front?' This was the first question the foreign journalist had asked them with genuine curiosity when he had landed at their base camp, travelling many days across the deep jungles and climbing the hills.

For the sole reason of forming a sovereign nation, or for self-empowerment, independence or some other personal reason? Lack of employment? Failure in love or heartbreak? A deep urge for adventure?

He grew quiet for some time. With slight hesitation, he asked himself, 'Did I actually go into the depth, search for that underlying truth and think about its impact while taking that decision?' The fire that was burning—actions and reactions, memories, history, rumours, folklore—had pushed him towards the hills. Small incidents and actions that propelled big reactions. At that moment he could recall just one thing. There was a solar eclipse on the day he had left. It was difficult to say whether it was morning or evening. The wind had brought along a germ that had caused irritation and burning in the eyes of the villagers. People's eyes had swollen and turned red. They christened this disease with a strange name, 'Jai Bangla'. Some said that the disease had first occurred at the time when the neighbouring country—Bangladesh—got its independence. Others said the migrants who had come from that country in the 1970s had brought the germs to this part of the world. Bidding his silent farewell to those who were suffering from that disease, he had left his village to climb up the hills. What exactly was the trigger point, he still had no clue.

Ignoring his silence, the intelligent young commando next to him started explaining their struggle in the context of geopolitics, sociology, economics and culture. His logical but ideological speech was drowned in the din of passionate words that came out of a lean boy as he countered the journalist with a question, 'Have you ever seen anybody pouring kerosene over her clothes and burning it? I have. I have seen my sister burning her torn, bloodstained attire. Limping around, her legs apart, she poured kerosene over the bundle of her torn dress. Her earlobe was torn, the lower lip was swollen, and the neck had teeth marks. Burning her dress, she went to the cowshed and looking at the black smoke that blew towards it, she babbled, "I am getting rid of the mosquitoes." She sat under the hand-pump, rubbing herself with a ridge-gourd loofah so vigorously that blood oozed out of her skin. She kept on rinsing herself, hour after hour. Nobody had the courage to tell her to stop, nobody had the courage to tell her that the dress was required as proof. Only a few heartbreaking words travelled from one end to the other in the form of whispers—there were three of them, three uniform-wallahs. When they could not find the underground people, they did her.' The boy who narrated the incident was barely out of his teens. Unable to withstand his bloodshot eyes, the journalist had lowered his gaze. For a few moments, he had looked down and played with his recorder, then fixing his gaze on the silent one, had asked, 'Don't you have anything to say?'

He suddenly recalled a small incident, his own experience of visiting the national capital to take the post-graduate entrance exams with a few fellow students. The moment they alighted from the train, singling them out of hundreds of passengers, a few men in uniform had dragged them to a secluded area. As they were checking their bags, throwing the contents everywhere, the loudspeaker kept announcing, 'Do not talk to strangers. If you spot any suspicious person, immediately report them to the police.' Did their crescent moon-like eyes and porcupine thorn-like hair make them suspicious characters? As those hands checked his body inch by inch, they groped the organ between his legs and broke into laughter—the little mouse was scared and had shrunk.

Understood, it was a humiliating experience, the journalist had said. However, was it strong enough a reason for taking such a drastic step? Surveillance is a part of modern civil life, an everyday reality. All minorities and marginalized communities are victims of this.

Though he did not reply, he was convinced that the hand that touched a sensitive nerve played its part in pushing him towards the hills. The hand with unlimited power that could put handcuffs or grope the part between the legs at will. And those hills—the agents of change—invited them in their embrace. While he climbed those steep slopes and crossed the dense forests with measured steps, his legs turned heavy and numb like ice, but his mind was free like a grasshopper's. It was filled with the possibilities that lay ahead. Akhai, walking ahead of him, had said with a hint of admiration, 'Some friends from the plains are so fragile—soft and delicate like boiled worms. But you are solid.'

Inspecting his middle finger, which was tough like steel, even Aathem had once said, 'Friend, you have steady hands. You can fire a perfect shot. You can handle a desi gun too. No matter how much of an expert you are at handling an AK-47, M16, G3, only if you know how to shoot a desi gun, are you a real fighter.'

He had wondered if he could become a real fighter. Could he fathom the definition of a real fighter, a real revolutionary? He recalled one night when he had come down from the hills and taken shelter in a house in the plains. The house was a bungalow in an old town built by the British, who had set up an oil refinery there. This town bore the old colonial flavour. Each alley, each house was reminiscent of the bygone Raj. The bungalow had a fireplace and chimney, mahogany flooring and a nicely pruned hedge. Climbing down the shining wax-polished staircase, he had crossed the kitchen garden and lit up a cigarette under the poma tree.

Looking at the picturesque scene with the fireflies twinkling in the backdrop of the velvety darkness of a moonless night, he did not have the heart to disturb the serenity with smoke. He moved a little further away by the poultry shed and puffed his cigarette. Frightened, the chickens inside started to cluck. A couple emerged from the hut. The woman said, 'Oh, not a jackal. We thought probably it was a jackal or *jahamal* looking for the fowl, but it's you, sir, you are our guest.' Their fourteen-year-old son had come out as well. In the light of the torch, he inspected him from head to toe. He said, 'Dada, please come inside. Come, I want to touch the thing on your waist.'

He was shocked. What was he to do? How sharp this teenager was! Spellbound, the teenager dragged him inside, touched the metallic thing and said, 'Ma, I will also go into the jungle when I grow up. Everyone will be afraid of me, and I will be allowed to stay in the bungalow of our sahib and will get to eat good food.'

He felt as if a python had struck him with its tail. Like a soldier retreating from the battlefield, he had moved back in a hurry. Climbing the stairs to the guestroom, he had banged his head in the darkness. The wife of his host stood before him. The host was away for work. She could not say no to his friend, so she had offered her guestroom to him for the night. With tired steps, she had come out to the veranda to apply moisturizer over her face and hands while enjoying the cool breeze. Leaning on the railings of the veranda, they stood in silence, admiring the bright stars scattered over the dark canvas. Looking at those stars, it seemed like some artist had allowed his unconscious mind to take control and throw those silvery drops on the canvas.

At some distance, a few mulberry trees were covered with brownish yellow blooms. There were mulberry blooms inside his mind too. Like the lid of an airtight pickle bottle, closed for years, that suddenly goes off, exposing the contents to the warmth of the sun, he started talking. He talked about anything and everything: From a baby elephant trumpeting for life after consuming a datura seed or those weird-shaped honeycombs on the branches of tall hizol trees in the deep jungles. He said that Bruce Lee was his favourite hero and pork cooked in castor and mashed potato in mustard oil and ginger his favourite food. He recalled that once, perched atop his maternal uncle's shoulders, he had gone to attend a Bihu function in the open field at night and sung Bhupen Hazarika's '*Manuhe manuhor babe/Jodihe okonu nebhabe* . . . If people don't think about others . . .'

She spoke as well. He asked her who her favourite writer was. She said there were many: Lorca, Neruda, Sylvia Plath, Akka Mahadevi, Anna Akhmatova, Kamal Majumdar, among others. He said those writers were artisans of words. Wordisans, he called them. Then she talked about Kabir Das. He had asked, 'Why don't you write a story about me or us?' After studying his face in the dark, she had said, 'Instead of spending the night here in this comfortable bungalow, had you gone to that hut or that labour colony or slept on the floor in one of those mud houses in the nearby village, I would have respected you more. Would that not be more appropriate considering the ideology you are fighting for and the dream you are nurturing?' For the second time, he was lashed by the powerful tail of a giant python.

Like she had said, their ideology and dreams were challenging. The journey embarked upon to attain those dreams was very tough. What had become much more challenging now was the return journey. Like those salmon. The salmon had already covered a long distance against the tide. Many of them had fallen prey to predatory bears.

He was also waiting. Waiting . . . waiting . . . like an inert body. Waiting in dilemma, doing the calculations—would he be a prey to bear-like entrapments or not? Syndicates, poaching, black market—each bear was waiting for him to make a move. The empire they had built on real estate—high-rise apartments, countless luxurious colonies like the Rang Ghar and the Talatal Ghar. Black Forest, Spanish Garden, Mountain Dew—those were the names of their kingdoms. The inhabitants of those kingdoms organized parties, which often turned ugly as the bloodthirsty goddess Ranachandi went for the kill after she had her fill with song, dance and other indulgences.

Those competitive buffaloes free of the rope and baying for blood would inevitably get into fights. They all were inhabitants of the same empire. They were the best of friends. Why did they turn into competitive buffaloes, like the ones in the Bihu fields? He had heard many stories of grass getting flattened under fighting buffaloes. Once, someone had trained his gun at one of his closest friends. Others had tried to separate them. Frustrated, he shot indiscriminately at the crows sitting on the electricity wire. One, two, three, four—they fell one after another. Immediately hundreds of grey and black crows circled the spot, creating a cyclone. Another surrealistic take on Van Gogh's *Wheatfield with Crows*. Only the one who created this scene was not Van Gogh. The creator of this scene was Picasso's wild, untamed bull in *Guernica*, which the artist had described as the centre of all darkness and brutality on earth.

Would he too end up becoming a bull? Would he book an apartment in that anarchist colony? His brother's voice and parody seemed to goad him, 'Go there, rather than puffing out smoke rings lying on the bed, go there.' His mother's voice came from within, 'Don't ever go away. Instead, go towards the pond, which is covered, go towards the riverbank, go watch those playful fish in the new pond.'

Exhausted and torn between the two voices, he would lie down. When his subconscious would find an escape in the bunker of sleep, that dream would grab him from behind. It was the recurring dream of the simolu tree.

Once, when he had crossed no man's land all by himself, to collect salt, he had lost his way on his return. Following the circuitous route that took him in circles like a man possessed, he had reached a small plain. The sun was sliding down the steep slope after a tiresome day's journey. The birds returning to their nests were shouting in unison—'farewell, farewell, farewell'. Amidst the hills, the plain resembled a round pan. There was a row of small huts. It was the colony of Wangsu Nagas. Seeing a stranger, they surrounded him, but as soon as they realized that he was from the camp, a fighter for independence, they respectfully took him to the village head's house.

A little distance away from the head's house was the *morungghar,* guest house. It was a beautiful house. At its entrance was a huge skull of a *mithun*. On both sides of the door were two huge deer horns. He was intrigued by the beak of the hornbill strategically placed between two spears and the intricate wood carvings on the pillars of the morungghar. The village head, who wore a string of five metallic skulls like medals, besides many other necklaces, asked him to spend the night on the floor of the morungghar. They made a huge fire outside. The five metal skulls were shining in the fire. He felt uneasy, as if those agents of death were smirking at him. The smirk of destiny. The well-toned, granite sculpture-like body of the village head, clad only in a loin cloth, a sharp knife by his side, and earlobes drooping with the weight of wild boar teeth, seemed like that of the messenger of death, the one ruling monarch in control of this entire primeval empire around him. The headman, pointing his fingers to a distant tree, said, 'Have you seen that simolu tree? That's where we hang our children when they die. If their spirits laugh and play at night, don't get scared, okay?'

He felt a chill course through his body. He stared at the simolu tree. In the backdrop of the darkness, it looked like a shadow moving towards the sky—a supernatural entity. Its branches were like hands, holding the bodies of the children, wrapped in cloth. Subjected to the scorching sun, wind and rain, those bodies would decompose and the flesh, skin and marrow would fall, bit by bit. Only the small skeleton and skulls would be left hanging there. Those skeletons and skulls would be brought down and buried, completing the final ritual.

He looked around himself and saw green grass, wild bamboo and corn patches.

The village head smiled, 'You must be wondering where we have buried those skeletons. Here, there—everywhere. It's no big deal. That's how they go back to nature.'

New life in the form of bamboo and wild corn would grow. This was the rule of nature.

Another cold wave washed over him. A gentle breeze from that simolu tree had touched him, licked his soul. In a semi-unconscious state, he had sat close to the fire for a long time. May be it was the hangover from the thoughts that played on his tired and anxious mind or some other reason, but that night he went through a strange experience.

At midnight, when he was hovering between consciousness and unconsciousness, dream and nightmare, he saw the tall simolu tree in the brownish yellow moonlight. Some children were chuckling as they played on its branches. With a set of transparent wings like those of a dragonfly's, they started flying. Making a wave in the air, they slowly descended. He realized to his horror that he was not sleeping on the floor of the morungghar, but on the grass in front of it. Flapping their dragonfly wings, the children started circling his body as they played in gay abandon. The cold breeze from their small wings touched his skin. Their transparent wings turned grey, and their laughter turned into stifled cries. They started sobbing and he woke up with a start. He found he was sleeping under the open sky in the pale moonlight. His body was covered with sweat.

The scene with the simolu tree got engraved in his subconscious. Everything else had evaporated from his mind except for that scene which, from time to time, in the form of a nightmare, grabbed him from behind. Ever since that day, he often imagined he had turned into a simolu tree with sobbing bodies of little ones hanging from his innumerable hands. He kept tossing and turning to break free from this nightmare, like a freshly slaughtered buffalo's jerking headless body drenched in its own blood. He forced himself to stay awake. Night after night he kept his eyes wide open.

He saw the salmon on his television screen had turned red. Blood red. A wave of warm blood that looked like a red river. The shoal had reached its birthplace. The fish were excited with the process of procreation on that flowing water table. The ultimate happiness of procreating had turned them red. That they would die shortly did not bother them. What else could beat the happiness that stemmed from coming back to the birthplace and giving birth to a whole new creation? Such a death was bound to be red. This red was different. This red was like the blood during menstruation. The red which brought with it the green seed of the future. He had found the answer he had been searching for the last five years, lying on the bed, making those smoke rings. He had to die like the salmons. The man within him, who was in a dilemma whether or not to fall prey to the gang of bears, would have to die. He would turn red in anticipation of the new beginning and a new person would have to be born. Many years had gone by simply trying to decide whether to jump or not to jump. Now was the time to make that leap.

Jumping up from the bed, he opened the door. Through that open door he left for the water-filled pond—stepping on the wet grass. The twilight when Hiranyakashipu's heart was shredded into pieces was long over and the fourteen-day-old moon had stepped into the sky softly. Like that old song, 'O moon, o my friend, today my moon is smiling, because tomorrow it will be full in the bright sky.'

The moon knew that after attaining its full size, it would start diminishing again and would have to complete another challenging journey. He looked at the wasteland around the pond stretching beyond the horizon. The wasteland stood like a knot of endless possibilities ready to untangle and unfold in his vision. Standing by the pond, he realized that he too would be getting ready to fight another battle like that moon of the fourteenth day. Would not the moon smile today? Would not this one, this very salmon standing by the water-filled pond, jump his final jump?

Epilogue

That night, he saw the recurring dream for the last time, the dream about the simolu tree. The dream appeared in an improvised form. This time he himself was hanging like a dead child. For decades, he was hanging from the branches of that kalbriksha or bodhibriksha, whatever you may call it—burnt in the heat, drenched in the rain, lashed by icy cold winds. The blood, flesh and skin of his physical body had decomposed. As if it was a cycle of purification. A journey of self-introspection. Stripped down to nothing but a handful of bones, he kept waiting for that final moment.

Under a blue sky, hanging from that kalbriksha, he kept waiting eagerly. The skeleton of his body would merge into the soil and the secret hymn of the universe would see that he was reborn as a bamboo or a wild corn.

Shark, Shark, a Huge Shark

In memory of the volatile days of the Assam agitation of the 1980s

First voice

Today is Chaturdashi, the fourteenth day of the lunar month. Tomorrow is Purnima, the day of the full moon. The full moon in the month of Chot, which means Hanuman Jayanti. There are many things to be done for the celebrations. We will all have to work as a team.

Today is Chaturdashi, for sure. The moon is not yet a complete circle. A small portion of it—not easily detectable—is yet to be rounded. It resembles an apple with a dent on one side.

I love eating apples. I don't like their taste; I find them a little sandy. But apples look beautiful, in their different colours—red, green, yellow. As beautiful as my mother. I love eating beautiful things like rosogullas. Rosogullas are like my mother, too. White and soft, sweet and juicy like my mother's words.

I am not being fed apples and rosogullas here. It is one dry roti or a little rice and one sabzi every day. They serve the same sabzi. The curry is bland and watery. The vegetable is a green fruit covered with thorny hair. We are also made to eat a dish made of a vegetable with rashes.

There is a beautiful hilly place I had been to once as a child. It was full of vines laden with those green fruits with rashes. Those creepers were all over the place, climbing the trees that lined the road and the boundary walls of the houses. How could those ugly fruits grow in such a beautiful place? What is likeable may not be completely likeable—like beauty may not be beautiful in totality, isn't it? I forgot to tell you that we are served dal too. I love the bowl in which the dal is served. I put my finger in the aluminium bowl and make it rotate. Reciting a mantra, I exorcise everyone who lives in the big hall. The way Sarat Dada had once exorcised me, with his index finger cutting through the water in a bell-metal bowl and his other hand thrashing me with a broom. Whenever I go to exorcise the fat uncle who sleeps in the bed next to mine, he makes a dash at me. He stinks of bidis. Uncle often puts his bidi into my mouth—where does he get his bidis from? He says, 'Puff monkey puff, take this prasad.' Taking a puff or two, I pull out a strand of hair from his bare chest. Grabbing my hand, he thrusts it under the lungi tied around his waist and says, 'Here, pull this one too. Here, here, pull it harder.' I pull it hard. Everyone laughs.

The math teacher does not laugh. The tall, lanky man, who paces up and down for hours together, does not laugh. The men chained to their beds at the other end of the hall do not laugh. The boy who is roughly the same age as me, the one who sits like a statue on his bed and stares out of the window, day after day, night after night, without changing his expression, does not laugh either. That thinker is a horse, like the horse carved out of stone in front of our Deoshal Shiva temple. The horse that can sleep while sitting, even standing. The stone horse that sleeps and, all of a sudden, wakes up screaming and sweating profusely. A chill goes down my spine, my heart beating like crazy. His screams are a battle cry, 'Come out, come on out. The enemy has arrived.' Shouting those slogans, beating gongs, dhols and bugle, they march on.

I understand why they cry those battle cries. I know everything, but I don't let people know what I know. Once they realize that I understand, they don't tell me what's on their mind. People open up only to those who do not understand anything. We pity those who are inferior to us. My mother had realized that I understood everything. Whenever someone spoke against me, she would shout at them, 'He knows everything. He understands. Didn't he stand first in his class? The rows and rows of books in that almirah, who do they belong to? Did he bring them for decorative purposes? All these stupid idiots are now laughing at my son—how dare they, how dare they?'

She would sob. How strange was my mother, like a small girl. So lovable, so beautiful. I would hug her tight, fish out a candy from my pocket and give it to her. Putting it in her mouth, she would stop crying. I would then pick up the bottle of coconut oil and a comb from her dressing table. My mother would look at me and smile. My mother was so beautiful—fair hands, fair feet and under that white chaddar, her fair belly. The only things I did not like on that beautiful tummy were some creeper-like scars around the navel. Not exactly creepers, more like a patch of white grass growing underneath a huge stone and crawling upwards.

'Oh God, ma, what happened?' Ma would reply, 'Oh those, those happened because of you. These are the signs that you came out of my tummy.' I would be angry at myself. My head would spin. 'What have I done? I caused a flaw on my mother's beautiful tummy. The one I love the most, I scratched her and gave her those scars. Had I not been born, her tummy would have been beautiful forever.'

On such occasions, my heart would be heavy with pain. My chest would be twisted in knots and my body would convulse as though thousands of needles had pierced it. I would sweat profusely, as if I was on fire. My body would go limp, hands and feet would shake, my vision would go blurry. I would not be able to breathe, feeling as if someone had kept a brick on my chest. My lower abdomen would hurt, and I would feel the urge to pee. The floor would rise and fall in waves, throwing me off balance. The hum of a thousand bees, thousands of different voices would assault my ears. Like the cacophony of thousands of terrified birds on that peepul tree during a solar eclipse, those voices would call me, 'Come, come out, come, come out . . .'

Third voice

Shattering the silence of the night, the battle cries came closer—the reverberating sound of thousands of voices, magnified by the trumpet, bugle, dhol and gong. There was a blackout. No light was allowed tonight, whether electric or earthen lamps. The march with the battle cries continued.

Disrupting the graveyard-like silence and piercing through the pitch darkness of the night, the battle cries came closer, 'Come on out, come on out! The enemy has come to destroy our land, come to the battlegrounds . . .'

With his tiny heart thumping in anticipation of something sinister, he reached for the small *muda* and dragged it to the window. Climbing onto it, he peeped out through the curtains. All he saw was an unending stretch of darkness, black as his mother's *mekhela* dress. Like her black tresses. Like the road he took to his school, freshly coated with tar. In that big bowl of darkness, amidst the reverberating sound of battle cries, he saw countless dots of lights coming towards him. Thousands of burning torches were moving in unison as they marched forward, forming a wave of lights.

He buried his head into the bosom of his mother who had tiptoed into his room and stood close to him. Such screams, such words used. His ears began to buzz. As the darkness blended with even darker tones, presenting a scary picture, the tiny soul, shivering from head to toe, clutched onto his mother's chaddar. His body jerked involuntarily, as if thousands of needles had pierced him. His ears were on fire, his body lost equilibrium, his hands and legs shook, it became difficult for him to breathe, as if someone had put a heavy brick on his chest, his lower abdomen and legs hurt, 'Ma, ma, I want to pee, ma,' he said.

Groping in the darkness, he tried to get out of the room, 'I am scared to go out alone, ma, the floor has tilted, it's going up and down . . . ' A stream of hot liquid trickled down his legs. Filled with shame, he tried to lift one leg and undo his pants, but, unable to find his balance, he collapsed on the spot. The sharp garlicky smell assaulted his nostrils. Like a toddler, he tried to crawl out of the room.

Most nights, he crawled on the floor. As night fell, he felt like he might fall off the surface of the earth. He would sit down and try to clutch onto the floor. The science teacher had said that the earth is round, and people inhabit the surface of the earth, like lizards climbing the wall. On this constantly revolving ball, like ants move without feeling the movement, people moved around not feeling the motion of the earth's rotation and revolution. What if he fell into that dark bottomless pit of space? The science teacher had said, 'That's impossible.' He now mouthed those words.

A beautiful word, but tough. The science teacher used tough but powerful words.

Among all these words, he liked 'impossible' the most. Just as the science teacher uttered that word, in his baritone voice with pride, he too uttered 'impossible, impossible', as he crawled on the floor at night.

As soon as night fell, weird things would start to happen. Those events took place in a muted manner during the day, but they came alive mostly at night, in quick succession. He did not tell anyone about them, except Bengi, the dimwit. The one who sat still on the last bench, the one whom everyone called names like Bhutni and Bengi, the one whom no one talked to, who did not play. Only Bengi listened to him, believed what he said. She did not laugh at him or mock him.

Looking deep into her eyes, he would tell her how as soon as night fell, the walls of his room would start weeping. The trees outside his room would knock on the window and call him out. The branches would come down and whisper about his dead brother and many others like him. The branches would whisper the names of those who had drowned or died in car accidents or of cholera. The dead children attended school, a night school. Admission was on a first died, first served basis.

The twinkling stars in the sky, which seemed to be smiling, were not smiling. They were quite lonely. They had no one. They had no companions, no brothers. Why did his brother have to die like that? Why did God take away his brother? Other children, too, had brothers. When his body was pulled out of water, it was swollen, filled with blisters, as if burnt. His eyes had been nibbled away by fish. When he saw the distorted, decayed body of his brother, the first thought that crossed his mind was that he was lucky it was his brother and not him. At the same time, his heart cried out for his brother. Suddenly, he was choking. As his heart started doing somersaults inside his ribs, he began sweating profusely, his ears began ringing, his head swimming, his hands and feet became unsteady and the floor underneath his feet started to slip away. He felt an acute pressure in his lower abdomen, and a warm stream of liquid threatened to come out. His brother's face, with both eyeballs nibbled away by fish, remained etched in his mind forever. Each night, sometimes through a nightmare and sometimes leaning on the wings of memory, those two eyeball-less eyes would pursue him, and he would scream wordlessly, 'Ma, ma, I am scared. Come to me.'

He knew his father would not allow his mother to come to him. Even though she slept next to him sometimes, later, when she thought he was asleep, she would tiptoe back to the next room, to be with his father. He knew because he only pretended to be asleep. When his mother would leave, he would plead with her silently, 'Ma, don't go away, the moment you leave, these walls start howling, the trees whisper about the school of dead children ...'

Once, after his mother left, he got up from the bed and silently stood close to the door. He gave an involuntary shudder as some unknown, intense dark feeling crippled his soul. Why was his mother whining like a puppy? Why was his father grunting like the pigs when they played in the slushy pond behind Bubul's house? Why did these things happen at night? Outside this house? Inside his house, in the next room?

He felt a surge of anger towards his father. He desperately wanted to hate his father. His father was meting out some sort of punishment to his mother. He dragged her away from him; his father had pushed him into a lonely world filled with fear. A world with a spinning floor, from where he could fall easily into a dark hole, a world where the walls wept bitterly, the trees had a rollcall of the dead children, and the sky was filled with lonely stars with fake smiles. In that world every brother was dead. In the daylight, however, when everything was radiant, transparent and beautiful, he was filled with shame. His love for his father once again resurfaced. Especially when he bought him rosogullas or apples. Apples are so beautiful— red, green, yellow.

He gazed at the apples, fiddling with them. Travelling thousands of miles in trucks from their place of origin, a faraway place called 'Heaven on Earth', the apples entered his state. In that snow-laden place, in numerous lakes, young children moved around in small boats called shikaras. If only he, too, could row a boat and leave this place.

If he left, would his mother not cry? If he left, never to return, his mother would go howling mad.

Like that time when his father went on an official tour for two days and did not return for a long time. Nobody knew where he was. His mother would pace to the bamboo gate and back. She would forget to put salt in the dal, and sugar in his milk. Dirty clothes remained on the bathroom floor for days and a dank smell rose from the heap. Hiding from him, she would weep and light diyas before the Charurbhuj idol in the temple.

The day his father had returned, in unkempt clothes and hair, dirty and tired, she ran to him and, in front of everyone, hugged him and cried. Though he was ashamed of her conduct and was irritated at her for holding on to his father so intimately, seeing his father he too felt like a kite. *Deuta.* Father.

Father was bedridden for quite a few days. He spent many a day hungry and sleepless, always anxious. Disruption of a railway track, bandh, blackout, battle cry, procession, curfew, abduction—what had happened to his father? He had no answer. Nobody told him. The bile was threatening to escape from his throat.

He was quite happy those days. Like a pitcher filled to the brim, he felt satisfied. The school was shut. His father was in the house. People would come to visit. They would sit around his bed, and, amidst a frequent supply of tea and malpua followed by betel nut and paan, they would whisper. Sometimes their decibel levels would rise out of anger, frustration and repulsion. He liked it, he liked it very much. Many tongue-twisting, heavy words were added to his vocabulary. Identity. Revolution. Martyrdom. Sacrifice. Martyrs. Bloodbath. Communal clashes. Public. Peace talks. Terrorism. Divisive forces. Ultras. Rape. Killings. Absconding. Miscreants. Bomb blast.

All these words would overwhelm him. Like a cacophony of birds coming back home, or a herd of goats caught in a thunderstorm and running helter-skelter, those hundreds of words invaded his consciousness in a rush, creating chaos, and his tired, paralyzed brain, unable to withstand their assault, would lapse into the surreal world.

The people said beware of them. Who were 'they'? He could not find an answer to that. How did they look? Were they like the monsters depicted in comics and storybooks? Did they sport two horns? Were they covered with hair?

Looking into Bengi's eyes, he said, 'These miscreants are roaming everywhere. They are amidst us, disguising themselves as human beings. They can be here too. In our class, sitting among us.'

Anil Kapoor Dada shouted at the top of his voice, 'There is a gathering, a huge gathering.'

He didn't know Anil Kapoor Dada's real name. Mandira baideo had once commented that he looked exactly like the Hindi film hero Anil Kapoor, and since then everyone called him Anil Kapoor Dada.

He had never seen Anil Kapoor because his father did not allow him to watch Hindi films. He had watched only two movies—*Mother and Love*, and *Dharmakai*. He hoped to watch Anil Kapoor or Amitabh Bachchan's movies someday.

He might not have had the chance to watch Anil Kapoor or Amitabh Bachchan, but he had seen a revolutionary or a rebel. Like Anil Kapoor Dada's 'gathering', the word 'revolutionary' or 'fellow rebel' too held a fascination for him. What would a rebel look like? How strong would he be? Probably he would wear black clothes, sport a long beard and a hood and his body would be robust and well-toned—like Babu Dada's.

One day, Bubul, the young boy from his neighbourhood, had whispered to him, 'A rebel is hiding in our house.' Thousands of volts of electricity ran through his veins, his young heart started beating wildly in anticipation of adventure.

Hopping and skipping with Bubul, he ran to face the much-awaited moment.

Peeping through the curtains in their guest room, he saw a skinny young man, who would be roughly Babu Dada's age. He was reading a newspaper. He didn't know why, but he was disappointed. He recalled what his science teacher had said, 'In that seemingly innocent atom lies the power to destroy an entire civilization.'

Perhaps the man in front of him was like an atom, full of potential. In the following four or five months, it became a ritual for them to silently observe the rebel with respect and admiration. They could see the rebel mostly doing two things—waking up late in the morning, eating a hearty breakfast and then lying on the bed throughout the day, lost in thought, or laughing and talking with Bubul's mother either in the bedroom or in the kitchen.

One day Bubul got a little miffed with his guest. His family had only one hen. She used to lay an egg every day and his mother used to fry that egg for Bubul. Over the last few days, his mother was giving that egg to the rebel. The rebel was used to a breakfast of four dry rotis, tea and a boiled egg. His father, who worked as a peon in a government office, could not afford to buy fish, meat and eggs every day.

While stating his egg problem, Bubul's eyes became teary. Unable to console his friend, he repeated the words that Anil Kapoor Dada had told his father, 'Sacrifice, sacrifice. We need to sacrifice. For the sake of peace and prosperity, we must be ready to make the supreme sacrifice. This is a question of our existence.' Failing to understand what was just said, Bubul looked lost and after a minute or so, he smiled and said, 'Let's go play.'

He had somehow managed to pacify Bubul on that issue, but another day Bubul came to him in tears. His sobs were punctuated by hiccups which almost paralyzed him. He goaded Bubul to speak out, 'Tell me, tell me na, what happened, speak up.' Bubul's tears, laced with pain, were spreading to his heart too.

Wiping the snot running down his nose with the collar of his shirt, and drying his tears with his tiny palms, Bubul said haltingly, 'Don't tell anyone, ok? Swear by Goddess Saraswati. Do you sometimes fondle your mother's breasts?'

Yes, he nodded after a moment of silence.

'It feels so good, right?'

'Yes.'

'Nowadays, my mother does not allow me to touch them. You know my mother is the angry type, but in reality, she is very good, very loving. She loves me a lot. When my father scolds her, then she gets angry. She takes out her anger on me. She hits me, scolds me and sometimes pushes me away from her. Once her anger subsides, she talks to me lovingly; she fries my favourite flat rice and does not scream at me when I touch her boobs. These days, I mean since last year, she scolds me whenever I touch them, "You are old now, almost eight, go away. Are you not ashamed of yourself? A class IV student. But . . ."' Bubul's voice trembled, the tone distorted like the sound of a broken *dotara*, 'But last evening, why did she allow rebel dada to touch them?'

Looking at his friend Bubul, who resembled a tiny, forlorn kitten with two big melancholic eyes, and listening to his voice, he realized something—it was not easy to untangle the knots between innocence, knowledge and revealed secrets. How unbearable was it to surrender in front of someone without any cover. To sit afterwards, head hung in shame. To look into someone's eyes with a face ashen with shame, guilt, helplessness and pain.

He stood before the ashen face of Bubul for a long time. The pain was contagious, like love or hate. The stream of pain from Bubul's heart drenched him. He was drowned in a fathomless well of pain. He felt his heart was being pressed hard by something, he was having difficulty breathing. With his heart pounding, he started sweating profusely. His ears started ringing, his hands and legs started shaking, his head began spinning and the floor started tilting in a wave. He felt a sharp pain in his lower abdomen and legs, and he began praying to Hanuman.

Jai Hanuman, gyan gun sagar
Jai kapis tihun lok ujagar
Ram doot atulit bal dhama
Anjaniputra pawan sutnama

In his mind's eye, he saw Anjaniputra Hanuman flying towards him, tearing clouds apart. His favourite god, the mythical man. He carried him and Bubul on his palm, whisked them off to a blessed land, wiped out their misery, just like he wiped off his cold sweat after a nightmare. With a swing of his mace, he shooed away the trees conducting a roll call of the dead students and silenced the whispering walls.

Whenever he would get scared at night, hearing the whispers of the trees and whimpers of the walls, he would grab a comic book from the bookshelf and read it under torchlight so that his parents wouldn't know.

He would have goosebumps reading about Yayati—what if his father too turned him into an old man in a quest for eternal youth? Why did Parasuram axe his mother on the command of his father Jamdagni? Why did Ram leave Sita all alone in the jungle? Reading all these tales, his tiny mind would be burdened with thousands of questions. The day the sky started firing shots and the stars were running helter-skelter, he came face to face with this divine figure on the cover of an *Amar Chitra Katha* comic book—half-monkey and half-human. Huge, with rippling muscles, more attractive than the hunk Arnold Schwarzenegger, whose poster hung on the wall of Babu Dada's room. What was more fascinating about this strangely good-looking God was his characterization.

The character gobbles up the sun and loses his powers after a rishi puts a curse on him. The rishi told him, 'The day it will be required of you, the divine powers will return, and you will be invincible.'

Later, his mother had narrated the tales of Hanuman to him—Hanuman carrying the Gandhamadan Mountain, Hanuman crossing the ocean with a single leap, Hanuman sobbing in front of Sita in the Ashok Vatika—so many shades to his character. His mother would also describe the festivities of the Hanuman Mela from her childhood.

'Such a variety of trinkets, recitation of the Ram Leela, a huge range of clay idols of Hanuman on display,' describing those scenes of the Hanuman Mela, his mother would get nostalgic. She once lamented to his father about how long it had been since she had gone to her mother's home. Almost ten years, that was before his birth. Next time they must go. His mother had promised to take him to his grandmother's house on Hanuman Jayanti and to the Hanuman Mela. On the full moon night of the month of Chot.

Corroborating his knowledge of the dark half and light half of the lunar months which he had learnt from his science teacher with the wisdom of his mother's *panjika* (almanac), he would assiduously track the moon—its shape and movement. When the crescent-shaped silver knife would take the shape of an apple with a dent on one side and when it would take the shape of his bell-metal plate, he would dream of coming face to face with the monkey god, whose touch would awaken his latent powers.

While this mythical hero took him from a perplexing world to a faraway dream-like place in his fantasies, Amanda used to tell him true stories about a dream-like place many nautical miles away. He had blended that world as well into his inexplicable, surreal one. Amanda was his pen friend, a resident of a continent where it would be night if it was daytime in his part of the world. He had never met Amanda, with whom he had exchanged letters for one complete year, but he could see her through her letters, sometimes he touched her. Those days came long after that painful, incomprehensible afternoon with Bubul.

It was Babu Dada who had introduced him to Amanda. The same Babu Dada had introduced him to a lot of strange things. He found her when he was battling with the complexities of his adolescent years. They had sent him a list of pen friends after Babu Dada posted four reply coupons of Amity International in his name by paying Rs 4 as postal charges. He had picked Amanda from that list.

Like the coaches of a moving train, years passed by. Like a train engulfed by darkness upon entering a tunnel, his life entered the tunnel of forgetfulness. The tunnel ended and once again light illuminated life and he stepped into reality with all its beauty and ugliness. Eluding memories, the inhabitant of a mentally disturbed, imbalanced world, that schizophrenic entity hung onto a few shadowy characters.

Scenes from the recesses of his memory, in bits and pieces, peeped into his subconscious mind—snapshots of a series of meaningful and meaningless scenes, the physical manifestations of which he had experienced so frequently in his childhood, sweating excessively, trembling, his head spinning. When he felt the floor beneath his feet slipping away and a sharp pain in his chest, he shook in anticipation of something terrible. All those things became an integral part of his being. Like the coaches of a train, years trailed one after another to become a decade, many lives like his, which germinated in the seventies and eighties and took root in the shades of anarchy, started growing like insect-infested, distorted fruits. With time, the chaotic existence became easy and looked ordinary. Like a blotting paper, blood absorbed that polluted anarchy. Like the thorny cacti of the desert that accumulates water, life went on, at a detached, silent and an unnaturally natural pace. Bubul, in the scheme of time, became a convict.

Like every other day, that day the tea vendor had told Bubul, 'How long are you going to sit idle and live off your old father? Why don't you ask your Minister Dada for a job? If he does not help you, who will? There is something called returning the favour. How long did he hide in your house? And your mother, how she took care of him.' Day after day, the same dialogue, the same meaningful smile. Picking up a butcher's knife from the slaughterhouse next door, he slashed the throat of the tea vendor in a single stroke. Gulping down his cup of tea, he dashed to the nearby police station. That was Bubul's story.

Babu Dada had left for Amanda's country forever. For a life of comfort and luxury which a multinational company in a country of a thousand skyscrapers could provide. Bengi—what had happened to her? All of a sudden, she started writing a story or two. Bengi became a writer. She discovered the first man from her childhood days, the one who had mesmerized her with hundreds of stories, on the floor of a big, long Assam-type house. An attending nurse was counting the number of men who queued up to step out for physical work and exercises and finally announced, 'All patients, in total seventy-six.'

He was sitting in the dank, unkempt corner bed of the hall. He was the same. With those lively eyes, he was looking at the sky through the window. He could still count the lunar days, Suklapaksha–Krishnapaksha, without a hitch. Looking at the movement of the moon and its shape and size, he could tell which day, which fortnight, which *tithi* it was.

First voice

Today is Chaturdashi. Tomorrow will be Hanuman Jayanti. We will celebrate Hanuman Jayanti. We will cook churma prasad—wheat flour, ghee, dry fruits, cardamom—we will make ladoo for prasad and I will break the coconut. Only men can break the coconut. I love eating churma and ladoo. Ladoos are round and beautiful. I love beautiful things. Those beautiful food items, their enticing aroma, bursting with flavour.

I will be calling a meeting for the organizing committee of Hanuman Jayanti. I have informed everyone. I want a big gathering on the day of Hanuman Jayanti.

The aroma of fried fish comes floating from across the wall. How long have I not eaten fish fry? I sing, 'Fish fry, fish fry . . . fry fry fry.' Hearing my song, kitchen uncle shouts, 'Wait, I will teach you a lesson, you son of a nawab!' All I am doing today is singing, because tomorrow is Hanuman Jayanti. I am happy. The fish fry song is picked up by all, even the ones chained in the corner. The chains are like anklets. They make a nice crackling sound. Everyone loves the song. Everyone loves to sing. Amanda, too, likes to sing.

When I hear a song, that song plays in my mind throughout the day. Since yesterday, it is the song, '*Saat samudrar parore, dhunia koi bazaar re, hatthi ki ghura ana, papa lakhmi aha na* [From across the seven seas, O father, bring me a horse and an elephant from that wonderful bazaar].' Amanda had come across the seven seas. I had shown Amanda the jar where I had kept my mother's clipped nails. The jar actually belonged to my mother. Ma used to keep her bindis, clips and a pair of earrings in it and called it the blue box. The day ma had died, I cut her nails with a blade. I knew she was going to die. Even ma knew that she was going to die. Her hair was constantly falling, the pate was visible, because of some intense rays which were made to pass through her body. Whatever was left, I used to oil and braid. Ma had said, 'My nails have grown so long.' To clip those long blue nails, I had brought a blade. When I took her hand to clip them, I felt how light her hand had become. Like a dry twig. Life is heavy. That's why when one is alive, one has weight. When life is drained out, the body grows lighter and lighter. Amanda fiddled with the nails and said, 'You are so handsome. Your mother, too, is beautiful.' I had replied, 'You too, Amanda, you too. Your mother is beautiful too.'

Amanda's mother had left her long ago. One day, returning from school, she found out that her mother was gone, only her red coat was hanging on the clothes hanger. Her mother had left with her lover to start a new life. That night, her father's friends came home to drink and dance, among them her father's would-be wife. Where was Amanda at the time? Wearing her mother's red coat, she was sitting on the stairs. The coat reached her ankles. I know what she must have been thinking. Ma knew that I know everything. I understand everything. I know from where the fat uncle gets his supply of bidis, who climbs on to his bed at night. I know that the bell is about to ring. We will stand in a queue and go outside to cut grass in the sun and clean latrines and drains. There are tender white worms in the latrines and black ones in the heavy black water of the drains.

It feels good to be out in the sun and work, the breeze touching the body. Even when my hands start hurting, I keep working. I love being outdoors. How beautiful the outside world is. We have meetings outside. If we make noise, the Main Sir comes running to us and says, 'Don't make noise. Work, work.' When I hear that, I feel like tickling his asshole with a blade of banguti, the itchy grass which I have just plucked. My mother used to say, 'One should not think badly of others.' Ma used to speak only of the good things. Amanda, too. How beautiful is the place where Amanda lives.

The names of the places in the country where Amanda lives are interesting. Like the names of some beautiful girls— Alabama, Carolina, Florida, Kissimmee. Amanda's mother was born in the house of a native Indian in Kissimmee. Amanda told me about the crack houses and about a Red

Indian warrior named Cockroach. Was Cockroach as strong as Hanuman? Yes, Amanda likes Hanuman too. 'Amanda, sweetheart, how do you know about Hanuman?' She had laughed out loud and said, 'My father was a hippie. He knew everyone—Buddha, Mahabir, yogis, Lakshmi, Saraswati, Durga, Hanuman. Among all the gods, I like Hanuman the most. I don't know why. Despite being such a strong, powerful entity, how could he be so humble? Despite being the most powerful, how completely he had surrendered himself to the love for Ram?' I liked Amanda because of her strange words.

When Amanda talked about Kissimmee, I loved it.

Such a beautiful name for a place, like kiss me. Amanda, she was always on my mind. Why, I can still taste her saliva! I sometimes ask myself: 'Why do I forget about my problems when I talk about her? When she is there, everything is. When she is not around, despite everything being there, there is emptiness. Why do I feel like talking about Amanda all the time? Why do I feel like telling everyone about her, even stopping strangers on the road and telling them—you love being by the sea, you like cacti, coleslaw and Coke and, like me, you like Hanuman too.'

Something is wrong at the organizing committee meeting for Hanuman Jayanti. The fat uncle said, 'Rather than organizing such *jayantis*, we should bring out a newspaper. I will be the editor.'

The three boys who were standing close to him started crying. These three cry at least four times a day. Who would bother with these crybabies? The tall, thin one, who keeps pacing up and down, kept on doing that. 'Go, yaar, who invited you to the meeting?'

'In this meeting itself the name of the newspaper should be finalized,' the fat uncle said. 'Usurped, usurped. A hundred quintals of milk powder and a hundred blankets have been usurped.' Yesterday, the math teacher had read out a news report that in the mental asylum, goods worth lakhs of rupees had been usurped—the fat uncle picked up the headline from there. The math teacher keeps doing sums and reads the newspaper aloud every day. A baideo always brings a copy of the newspaper for him.

When our newspaper is out, I will write about the shark. A true story. Amanda's grandfather was a hunter. He caught many big fish and alligators in the lake. In her childhood, Amanda's grandfather took her to the sea. He told her many stories about whales and sharks. One day, while sailing in a fishing boat, she saw a huge shark. A great white shark with a conical mouth where thousands of white teeth sparkled, and the fins were like the crescent moon. The sharks attacked the boats and ships. The floor of the ship swayed in the waves. The boats lost their balance. A huge killer shark came towards them. A grey, slightly bluish shark. Shark, shark, a huge shark. I have seen that shark in my dreams. Bubul and I were sitting on a boat and that shark attacked us. The water was not that of an ocean, it was the muddy water of the Pagala river where my brother had drowned. I screamed in my dream—shark, shark, a huge shark.

The man who screams at night, screams once again. I know why he screams at midnight, to fight for his rights. Newspapers are good. They have all my favourite words. The words which have been playing in my mind since my childhood. Terrorists, struggle for identity, rape, peace talks, human rights, rebel, revolution, migrants, displacement, son of soil, etc.

I felt angry. The meeting had been called for Hanuman Jayanti. Not for starting a newspaper. Tomorrow, I will break a coconut and pray, and Hanuman will come. The latent strength inside me will come out. Amanda will come as well. Amanda likes Hanuman too. The moment Hanuman comes, I will make everything all right with my power.

I will stop hearing the voices of the trees, I will no longer hear the rollcall of the dead children, nor the sobbing wall. I feel the excitement bubbling inside me. I swing the *dao* with which I prune the grasses, in the air, reciting the Hanuman Chalisa. Come Hanuman, come to my life. Everyone starts running helter-skelter.

The screams start echoing in my ears again. Gong, *doba*, cymbals and the war cry of thousands of people. Like the piteous cry of thousands of crows circling the old peepul tree during a solar eclipse. 'Come out, come on out . . . the enemy has come, come out.' I start sweating profusely, my ears start ringing as if thousands of needles have pierced my body. I feel a heavy weight on my chest, I cannot breathe. Convulsing, with foggy vision, I see the earth moving. It tilts to one side and then to the other. The floor is like a wave. I am going to fall off the ground, down, down into the dark hole. I feel an urgent need to pee. I try to run someplace safer. Someone comes running and pins my hands down. I cry out feebly. 'Today is Chaturdashi, tomorrow is the full-moon night of the month of Chot. Tomorrow my latent strength will come out. Tomorrow Amanda will come. Tomorrow I will come face to face with Hanuman.'

Third voice

The stout young man lying unconscious on the grass outside the asylum was dragged into a room by a doctor and a few nurses. Because of the sudden aggression, he was transferred to an isolated room, adjacent to the hall. The tranquilizers took effect and he fell into a deep slumber. The night of Chaturdashi passed by.

When he woke up it was the full-moon night of Chot Purnima. Opening his eyes, he saw a damp, moss-covered wall and a broken window. Resting his head on the cold handle of the folding bed, he looked out of the window.

His eyes popped out. Shock ran through his veins. There was a tall boundary wall and covering that wall was a huge tree with branches all over. He had never seen this wall before. On one of the branches was a red-faced monkey. His shining golden hair was dancing to the light breeze. He thought, 'Oh Almighty, so much like the monkey that had arrived before a sobbing Sita in the garden of Ashoka. Throwing a ring that carried hope and possibility.'

Surprised, mesmerized, and overcome with emotion, he kept looking at the monkey. A police van entered carrying a convict with a life sentence for murdering a tea vendor in the nearby town. At the same time, signing a special permission letter, Bengi opened the door of that isolated room.

The boy who was looking at the red-faced monkey for his ring of hope was startled by the sudden clatter at the door. Eyes wide open and heart beating wildly, he saw Amanda, whom he met only in his dreams, walking into his life.

Khanjar-e-ishq: A Filmi Kahani

Another story for those who still believe in love

'You are back?'

'Ummm . . .'

'Will you have a cup of black tea?'

'No.'

'Why? Have some.'

'Nah. I will sleep. I'm tired. I stumbled and hurt my toe. You cannot see anything so early in the morning. The streetlights were covered with fog. I walked fast and the wind! Like a whip it lashed . . . penetrating my bones.'

'That's why I tell you . . . leave it na. Leave it, leave it, I am pleading with you.'

'Again? You have to start all over again? Every morning it's the same. Stop nagging. It's of no use. Let me sleep in peace for a while. I was awake the whole night. Listen to me. Don't get angry. It's not going to be forever. Everything is coming to an end . . .'

'Yes. Everything is coming to an end—everything.'

'You have dragged yourself into this again, you bastard! Why do you keep repeating the same thing? Go, die . . . such negative words!'

'I am dying. A little bit every day. Those maggots are eating out my liver like ants nibble at sweets.'

'Stop that nonsense. Stop your melodrama. If you have nothing to say, stuff your mouth with cow dung. Let me sleep. I am dead tired, yaar . . . Let me lie down at least.'

'Lie down. Who is stopping you? I have kept the bed warm for you. I have burnt the coal, too. Look at the embers—red hot. Even the hot oil with burnt garlic cloves is ready for you.'

'What? You have again wasted garlic by burning it in oil? You dog! The price of vegetables is skyrocketing, and you are wasting garlic for a massage—I don't need your massage. What makes you do such things every day, huh? Some spirit possesses you or what? You yourself are in tatters—unsteady on your feet, no control over your limbs, screaming in pain. Look at you, looking like a worn-out plastic tent in one of those government night shelters, and you are coming to give me a massage—you will fall someday, you idiot . . .'

'You will love that. You are waiting for that only, you bitch. You are waiting for the day when I go down like a government night shelter tent so that you can savour dal makhni and tandoori chicken. You will wear a red zari saree and do *thumka* with some other man, you *chhammak chhallo* . . .'

'I will. Thousand times I will do that. Are you expecting me to go to the bank of the Ganga and die there? My foot! Listen to this, doggy: I am waiting for him to die—that's why I have been making trips to that fucker's faram house every night.'

'Oh yeah? I know everything. You have become a martyr— Nirupa Roy! Calling him a sadist! Who knows fucker or lover? Lover boy Salman Khan? Who knows that you are not having fun with that fucker? That thought does not allow me to sleep at night. I spend the whole night tossing and turning. I burn in hell's fury. Images of you with him . . . That bastard switching on the blue lamp, playing English music, playing a film on his big TV screen and looking at those men and women in action, while playing with you too . . . '

'Shut up, shut up, you dog. Bastard! Why are you killing yourself imagining all that? Stop, stop thinking. Peleeze . . . I'm saying peleeze . . . you should not think . . . should not . . . what is the alternative? What would you gain? Why do you hurt yourself?'

'You are hurting me, *haramzadi*. You are stabbing me with a knife day and night. You are bleeding me dead. You are putting those burning embers in my heart. You are pouring hot oil over me, you cunt! Who asked you to do this? Even if I did ask you to go there to save my life, why did you go? Why did you not say no?'

'What was I supposed to do, huh? Tell me, what was I supposed to do? What have you done? Where did you go? Who all did you approach? Did you fold your hands in front of anyone? Did you grovel at anyone's feet? *Saala*, you call yourself a man, huh? What else could I do? How else could I collect one lakh to save your miserable life? Washing utensils at people's houses or plucking eyebrows of those madams at some beauty parlour? Doing *pico* work at some tailor's shop? Which job would have helped me earn that much to save you, huh? If you are so miserable, why don't you leave home and go away? Why don't you die in front of a train in Shahdara?'

'I am dying. What life is this? Every day I die a little. Every night as I shiver in this cold, I burn inside thinking what all you would be doing. You spend the nights in comfort compared to me. At least you get to sleep on Dunpol . . .'

'Not Dunpol. Dunlop.'

'Whatever, teacher. Call it Dunpol or Dunlop. It is, after all, a soft mattress. Not like this old lumpy one. You have fun in the hot air from the heater. Unlike me. I have to keep blowing at the embers the whole night and sleep like a coiled-up millipede because the thin, torn blanket is not enough . . .'

'You don't need to. From today you don't have to sleep like a coiled millipede. Come with me tonight. Come and sleep on the floor in the heated room and watch how much comfort I have at night. How much fun I have, how much of a Salman Khan-type lover boy he is. How he showers his love on me. Come and witness how this lover of mine ties up my legs with chains. How he puts handcuffs on my hands, how he puts a leash around my neck and drags me around . . .'

* * *

'Oye, oye! Look, I'm holding my ears to apologize. Don't cry, please don't cry like this. I swear on my mother. I understand everything, I understand what torture you go through. That's why I burn like this. That's why I fight as soon as I see you. Everyday a new Kurukshetra . . . but don't I heat up the oil for a massage? Don't I keep the coals burning for you? But woman, my head also turns into a red-hot tandoor. Look what has happened to me. What sin had I committed that Yama's crab grabbed my liver? With this body, I drove a truck, crossed the borders like a bullet and delivered the *maal*, loaded and unloaded, carried heavy sacks over my shoulders, and now this body has become a sack with holes. Everything is over, woman, everything is over . . .'

'Now what? You stop me from crying and you are howling like a woman! Stop crying now. Am I working every night for nothing? Only a few more days. Three hundred per night. If I work for this amount for a while longer, we can have enough for the first instalment.'

'What if the maggots eat up my liver before that?'

'Keep quiet, you donkey. Keep quiet. They won't. They can't. Have I not told you? Even the doctors have said so. The moment we have the money, the doctor would burn out those maggots with hot air from a machine. *Saala*, they will burn in hell's fire . . .'

'Arre, wait! There are some burn marks on your back! Hey Ram! On the waist too and, and below that . . .'

'Oh, those. Those are from cigarette butts. Forget it. Just don't apply hot oil on them. It stings. Maybe some cold oil or ointment will give relief. Or just blow into them . . . slowly, yes. . . slowly.'

'Like this?'

'Yes, yes. S . . . l . . . o . . . w . . . l . . . y. Ummmm . . . that feels good . . . yeah g . . . o . . . o . . . d.'

'Hmmm.'

'Ummm.'

* * *

'He hehehe . . . '

'What he hehe? Why are you giggling, you monkey? Keep quiet.'

'He . . .'

'What, mad woman! Do people giggle at such a moment? Shut up . . . keep quiet na!'

'Why do you make a noise like a pig? How can I stop laughing? Like a pig makes that *ghut-ghut* sound after rolling in slush . . .'

'You mean to say I am a pig?'

'He . . .'

'Seriously, I have become a pig. Mud-covered pig. How dirty I am!'

'Again, you have started off. For how long will you keep dragging the same topic day and night, round and round like a jalebi? Drop it now. Let it go. And how are you dirty? I am the one who is dirty!'

'Arre, how can you be dirty? I am the dirty one. I pushed you towards dirt. Such a coward I am! I am so afraid to die that I send you there to die every day. I told the truck owner, "The crab got me. I served you for so long, now help me out." But what did the bastard say? "I will help but send her to me." And what did I do? I was so afraid to die and was so greedy for life that I asked you to go. I pushed you into the mud. I am the sinner. I made you dirty.'

'Huh. That means you really think I am dirty, right?'

'Arre, what are you babbling, woman? When did I say you are dirty?'

'You did. Just now you said it. First you said I am not dirty, but in the end, you said you made me dirty. That means you think I am dirty. Of course, you do. It is in your mind. Otherwise, why would you speak about it. Yes—I am dirty, dirty, dirty.'

'No, no. I don't think that way. Never.'

'You do. You do. A thousand times you do.'

'No. No. No.'

'Yes, you do. And I know for sure, and rightfully so. The day you become okay, the day you are not lying in bed like this, not limping around on unsteady feet, you will change. One day you will leave. Some clean woman will pull you towards her. You will lie to me and act, but in reality you will go away. Your body will be with me, your mind will go far away, drifting . . . and one day both the body and mind will be gone. You will run away. I know that for sure. You will run away. Men stay for a while and then they run away. That's how they are. It's in their nature to go for variety. Like honeybees . . . No, men are like flies. Flies that hover around filth. Or a stinging wasp . . .'

* * *

'What happened? How come there is no answer? Why are you quiet now?'

* * *

'What happened, O quiet one? Answer me. Say something. Are you admitting that what I am saying is true?'

'Hmmm . . .'

'Why are you not saying anything, bastard? That means you will leave? I am right, yes? Are you afraid that I know the truth?'

'Not true. But sometimes I am just afraid that it might turn out to be true. Like I am afraid every night that you might not come back in the morning. I think sometimes, why did you obey my command? Why did you go there to save me? Why did you not let me die? And if this fear is in your mind, why are you still trying to save me? Or are you in love with him?'

'Why would I let you die? Do you take me for such a loose woman? How could you even think that because you will leave me someday, I will allow you to die? That's how much you understand me! You think I am such a low-grade woman?

And if I let you die, if you must die, why would I deprive myself of the pleasure of killing you? I will kill you myself. You will die by my hand. I will chop you into two. I am not afraid of going to jail. But for the time being, go on living. We have been together for so long like man and wife, surviving through thick and thin. This is a bad phase. There is no need to look for the good, the bad or the ugly. This is not the time, there is no way out. The only thing that matters is survival. We need to cross this river. How we cross it is not important. Swimming or rowing a worn-out boat is not the issue. The aim is to cross the turbulent water and touch the ground. That's it. Final.'

* * *

'What happened. You are not saying anything. Why are you so quiet?'

* * *

'Arre, what happened? Why have you gotten up? Where are you going? Are you scared? That I will chop you up? Nah. Not immediately. Only if you leave me. Just kidding. Is it forbidden to kid around? Aye . . . what are you doing in the corner? What are you searching for?'

* * *

'Arre, come na. What are you looking for? What treasure have you buried there?'

'There is something. An object which I have treasured for a long time. The only gift that I got in my entire life.'

'Only gift, ha? What happened to all those gifts I gave you? Hankies, shaving creams, wallet? Once I gave you a vest too.'

'You call those gifts? I also gave you nail polish, bangles, lipstick, bra—flowery, lacy bra. I keep giving you things. These are things a man and a woman give each other. What's the big deal about these? This is called a gift. True stuff. Pure gift.'

'What? Let me have a look.'

'Here.'

'What kind of a gift is it? Who gave it to you? When? Why? Who gives such type of gifts?'

'Years ago. It was early morning. A foggy one like today. One could barely see what lay at an arm's distance. But if you need to answer nature's call, you have to answer it. One has to get out of bed, go out to the thicket or the railway tracks. Carrying the mug of water, as I was walking towards the tracks, I saw the morning Shatabdi train passing through the fog at full speed. Walking a little further, I reached the patch of vacant plot that has those thorny khar and babul trees. That's a nice area to relieve yourself. People don't notice you and water is available from a broken pipe. As I was just about to squat, I saw that a few shadowy figures, under the blanket of the fog, were wrestling with one another. A young voice was crying, pleading with them to let him go. Running to the spot I saw four or five people dragging a thin body. This is back when I had a body that could carry a two-ton sack, a big robust body with muscular arms and thighs. Not stopping to think even for a second, I jumped on them whispering "Jai Bajrangbali". Kicking and punching, it did not take me long to shoo them away. I hit the head of one of those with the gunmetal mug. Everyone ran for their life like the Shatabdi train that had disappeared into the fog.

'Chasing them for a while, I came back to the thin body, who was now sitting on the ground and crying uncontrollably. His face was swollen, and he was bleeding from the mouth and the nose. Pulling him up close, I saw that the puny body belonged to a child, just about twelve or thirteen years of age. By then I had forgotten the business that I had come there for. Picking up the boy in my arms, I started walking along the railway track. Following his directions, which he managed to convey in a feeble voice, we reached the Mughal Basti. Shouting "Ya Allah, ya Khuda", the distressed soul that came out of the door was another one in a pitiable condition. The old man was in his seventies or eighties. Seeing the condition of his grandchild, he sat down, trembling. After trembling for the time that one needs to chew and finish a Benarasi paan, he regained his composure. Pulling up the sleeves of his tattered kurta and dirty pyjamas, he stood up and poured water in a huge metal glass. Someone from the crowd that had already gathered there said, "Nanujaan, luck was on your side today. He has come back from the grip of the mafia of the sugarcane plantations." I had guessed it right. Such things do happen. Are you aware of such incidents?'

'What incidents? The sugarcane plantation mafia? Who are they? What do they do?'

'What? You don't know? Why, across the border and in the hinterland, sugarcane cultivation is done on thousands of bighas of land. Where do you think the labour comes from? From places like ours, they abduct young boys. They target boys from five–six to sixteen–seventeen years of age. They keep them in captivity for some time. There are security guards carrying loaded guns and knives round the clock. They catch those young ones because they cannot fight back.

Once trapped, they cannot come back and for their entire lives they work as bonded labour. They are made to work day and night in lieu of two chapattis twice a day and a chunk of jaggery.

'Hey Ram! What are you saying? Bonded labour? They work their entire life without getting paid? Such things are happening in this world even after the angrez have left our country?'

'Yes. Such things have been going on. So many children disappear every day. They just vanish and their poor parents cannot do a thing about it, except for beating their heads on the wall and dying.'

'Why do they not complain to the police?'

'Why do you always talk like an idiot? Will the police help the poor from the slums or those sugarcane planters who pay them thousands of rupees as *hafta*?'

'Oh God! They catch the young ones! Their life is worse than the lives of women like us. They must be torturing the captives!'

'Of course, they do. Things like beating or tying them up are very normal.'

'That's why they caught Nanujaan's grandson?'

'Yes. Usually during the midday and evening they are out on the prowl. But mostly they come early in the morning to the railway tracks, thickets, ponds and old ruins where people come to relieve themselves. That's where the *gundas* attack like wild dogs. It is easy to catch a young fellow while he is answering nature's call. It's easy to overpower them when they are in the middle of it. That's exactly what had happened to Nanujaan's little one.'

'God! But then, what did Nanujaan say to you?'

'To come to that, I had to narrate the whole incident. After drinking water, I was about to leave when Nanujaan called me inside. A small one-room hut, like ours. Nothing much inside, except for a wooden bed, a rickety chair and a corner table. There were a couple of shining brass vessels. They looked antique, with a Mughalia look. He handed me this one. I had never seen anything like this before. What shape, what weight, what workmanship!'

'Right, so beautiful. What intricate work. A royal one.'

'Have you noticed the *minakari* work? It's a gold-polished, genuine Mughal antique. It could be from Persia. Have you noticed its arch? Fit to test one's neck. Crooked head.'

'Ahh.'

'Ha. Now listen to what Nanujaan said. He said that this thing belonged to his forefathers. It was passed down to him through generations. Nanujaan belonged to a warrior family. This thing was from the time of King Zafar or even before. The Mughal era was over, so was the Raj. Nanujaan had lost everything, except for his grandson and this *khanjar*, which is actually a waist knife, small but sharp. To express his gratitude for saving the only lineage of his family, he gave it to me. The seventy or eighty-year-old man from the Mughal warrior family had tears in his eyes as he said this—this belongs to you from today.'

'Wow. What a beautiful story. Hope you have not made this up to please me! But why did you not tell me about it earlier?'

'Just like that.'

'You are so good. You saved someone's life.'

'I am no good. I did that without thinking. I was in my prime. When I saw that scuffle, I couldn't stop myself.'

'That's not true. After the fight you took the boy to Nanujaan. You did not leave him there to die bleeding. You are a good man. I will say this a thousand times.'

'No, woman. I am really bad. You don't know me. I have never told you all this because men do not talk about such things to a woman or in front of a woman. Men discuss things only with men. Men only love women, they play with women, those ticklish games.'

'You shameless man. But tell me, why are you bad?'

'Very bad. You don't know what all I transported to faraway places. Buried in the rice and wheat gunny bags, I smuggled white powder pouches, long arms, ammunitions, what do you know? Sometimes women, mostly girls. They would thump their chests and cry at my feet to let them go, "Bhai, you are like my brother, uncle, please save me." My heart never melted. "Shut up, rotten bitch," shouting at them, I supplied them across the border.'

'What? I spit on you.'

'That's why the crab got my liver. I have sinned. They cursed me.'

'Then why did the motherfucker truck owner not get this disease? He is the real sinner. He sent that stuff—those young girls. Why has nothing happened to him?'

'Why, I conned you too into running away with me. You were so happy in that faraway hilly place. Your native hills and people were so good and such simple folk, trusting everyone, offering every stranger a cup of black tea. And what did I do? With lies and false promises I got you in my truck and made you leave home. I told you I had a nice house and land. Even the truck was mine. After coming here, you saw it yourself, I am a creepy-crawly from hell.'

'I also kind of liked you. With you I did not mind living even in a stinking drain. You know what? I loved the smell of you. Your body smell can make me like . . . like . . .'

'Thank you.'

'Ishhh . . . ha ha . . . thank you!'

'I had my eyes only on your body, honestly. I didn't much care about your mind or heart. Your body could give me a high like Afghani charas. I wanted you, I wanted to maul your body and play. I have been to many parts of the country, but had never seen a woman like you before, the golden hue of your flesh, so tender and soft like butter made of purest buffalo milk, your long black tresses, like the darkest castor seed of the world, and your eyes! They were so different from all the women I had met and played with before, half-open half-closed as if eternally in meditation . . . ha haha . . . *chinky chinky meri jaan* . . . my friends would tease me. Where did you get this *chini mohini*? They doubted if you were desi maal for they had no idea that your hills are a part of our country too. Anyway, that thought of playing with your body day and night had driven me mad and I wanted to make you sit in my truck by hook or by crook. If needed I would have kidnapped you at knife point . . .'

'What? What did you say? Bastard! Wait, wait for a second. That was the reason you never told me about the khanjar, right? A genuine antique, *khandani* khanjar which you can use to stab, scare or abduct people right? Tell me something—you tell me every day that you are scared that I might not leave his side and come back in the morning to you or run away with another man. If something like that happens you would put this khanjar on my neck, right? Tell me honestly.'

* * *

'Answer me.'

'That's not correct. When I was diagnosed with this disease, and we ran short of money and my sadist owner asked me to send you to him, I went mad at the thought of dying. I thought if you did not comply or tried to run away, I would threaten you with this khanjar. But the whole thing took such a different turn. The moment you heard about my disease, you passed out like a chick fallen from a tall tree during a storm. You rolled on the floor, howling, and without uttering a word, you gave your consent for such a major step. I had imagined you would say no, you would charge at me, you would leave me—but no. You did nothing of that sort. Why? I go mad thinking why you did not protest. I feel you have kept a khanjar hidden within your chest. With that khanjar you are killing me every day. Now, if you stay at that fucker's faram house or go to some other man, I will not do anything. I don't have the right to stab you with this khanjar. No right at all.'

* * *

'Why are you looking at me like that?'

* * *

'Don't look at me like that. Like a pregnant cow. I am not done talking yet. I have not done any good deed in my entire life. I did only one. I saved Nanujaan's grandson and for that he gave me this medal. Today I am giving it to you. This is from me to you.'

'What? What would a woman do with a khanjar?'

'If I die, find yourself a good man. You can stay as that fucker's keep, but the moment he has had enough of you, he will throw you out.'

'What rubbish are you uttering, you bastard. Shut up. Find a good man. What good man are you talking about? How many of them are around in this world? Everyone is an opportunist. And when they get to know that I am a tank which had been muddied by two male buffaloes . . .'

'Wait na. Let me speak. Did you not say just a while ago that you would kill me if I ever left you? If I become all right and do such a thing, put this khanjar around my neck. I have given you permission. If necessary, I will give it in writing. Take it, take it. Hold it tight. From now on, this khanjar is yours . . .'

* * *

'What? Why are you staring?'

'Ha hahaha.'

'Why is this funny?'

'Because it is funny. You are so filmy. You are just uttering filmy dialogues. You must have gone for a movie last night with Banbihari, right? You must have had *daru*, you bastard. How many times the doctor has asked you not to—such a frightening disease you have and not giving two hoots, you have been drinking with Banbihari. Bastard. I could smell it. Tell me which film did you watch last night? *Jalim Jawani* or *Badan Main Aag*? Or *Rasili Raslila*?'

'Bitch, I did not watch any movie, neither am I mouthing filmy dialogues. I meant everything I said. You can kill me with this khanjar if I ever do any hanky-panky.'

'Wait! What was the first film that we watched together? *Salam-e-Ishq*? The salute of love! Listen, you also make a film. You will be the hero. A truck driver hero. I will be the heroine. A girl from a hilly village who elopes with him. The motherfucker truck owner is the villain. Banbihari will have a side role. Our own story will be the plot. In the end the hero will give the khanjar to the heroine and say, "Kill me, beloved, kill me." The heroine will say, "No no!" She will throw the khanjar away and say, "*Tere mere beech mein yeh khanjar nahi, pyar ki meethi chhuri ho.*" There will be no khanjar between you and me, only love. A love which is like a sweet stabbing knife in the heart. At the end they will hug each other tightly and kiss.'

'What will be the title of the film?'

'Why? Like *Salam-e-Ishq*, our film will be named Khanjar-e-Ishq.'

'Ha . . . good, very good! The film must have music. Who will provide the music?'

'Who else but Benarasi? Does he not sing kirtans every morning and smoke the chillum at night? He dances to all sorts of tunes. Just think of the devil and he has started off. There he goes with his kirtan and his dholki.'

'He is playing a *khanjari* and *tambura* also. There must be some festival today.'

'Whatever kirtan he sings, it sounds good, right?'

'It does. It sounds very good.'

'Listen . . . Today he is singing a strange song. Listen to what he is singing, his voice reverberating with a mesmerizing melody. . .'

A flower is blooming in Vrindavan,
But this is a strange one,
Is it blue, white or pink?
Nobody knows,
It blooms after twelve or 1200 years,
Today is that day,
Nobody can see that flower,
Except for two crazy souls,
Today that flower has bloomed early in the morning.

The Primitive Prayer

Dedicated to all the folk singers of the North-east and the world

The story of a song

As the eyes of the tiger shone menacingly in the dim moonlight, the song came to Momoko's lips, sprouting roots, slicing through her frozen heart. The eyes of the tiger were lit up and little Cheng in her lap was howling. The fading moon, suffering from insomnia, was panting with exhaustion when Momoko delivered the song.

Momoko's song was not a sweet one. It was salty, like a concoction of tears and blood. As she was singing, in her mind a face mauled by the tiger was floating away, and Cheng had fallen on the dark bed of sleep.

The static city on both sides of the highway was also turning in. Nobody had to sing a lullaby. There are no lullabies for cities. For the city, the nights are filled with the gurgling sounds of trucks and the screams of horns and sirens. Manoeuvring through this cacophony of barks, gurgles and screams was the Sumo Grande. There was no trace of sleep in the eyes of its driver. They were alive with the excitement of being on the verge of breaking a sensational story. A story about a song.

Is there a dearth of stories in this world? Sometimes the narrator chases a story and sometimes it's the other way round. In this backdrop of chasing and being chased, in the threshold of sleep and awakening, the driver of the Sumo Grande was moving towards the source of the story of the song. He had only one day in his hands.

* * *

Everything had to be completed within the next twenty-four hours. Spitting out the cigarette butt, he fiddled with the lights—high beam, dipper, high beam. Sometimes, there was hope from the high beam. Mostly, a feeling of despair carried by the shadow of the dipper. Would that woman listen to him? How far had he to go?

The restlessness originating from anxiety could not be soothed even by the luxe interior of the Ford Icon. Shaking it off with a conscious effort, he focused on the GPS system of the car. Driving through the smooth four-lane highway and onto the winding hilly road, he still had to travel quite a distance to reach his destination. Had it not been for the order of his guru, would he have come on this dangerous hilly road? Unless it was a do-or-die situation, who would do it?

He should have been travelling on a different one, the most prestigious, luxurious road on Planet Earth. This road, however, zig-zagged across futuristic ultramodern structures in the busiest city of the world across seven seas and thirteen rivers. He was to participate, along with his guru, in the international spectacle that would take place the very next day.

In his mind, the driver of the Ford Icon could see the snapshots of the glitziest event which would soon unfold in front of millions of spectators: A bright velvety, shiny red carpet. He visualized a man treading on it, as multicoloured laser beams created patterns on the carpet and a catchy tune played in the background. Onto the decorated stage arrived an impressive persona, sporting a fine, long salt and pepper beard and an even longer ponytail. He bowed slightly with the burden of unlimited talent and creativity. It appeared as if the owner of the lean body was accepting the reward of his lifelong meditation with grace. He had done much in the search of roots, restoration of heritage, assimilation of folk culture into global culture, strengthening of world peace and brotherhood through music. His unique creation symbolized all that and more, which was why the world's highest musical honour was being bestowed upon him.

These had been the headlines running for the past few weeks. He was the musical guru—world-famous singer, composer, lyricist and music director. The occupant of the Ford Icon had received his training under him. He was now the lead vocalist of his guru's band. He felt a rush of pride and the mental picture of his guru under the spotlight and its bright surroundings lingered on.

* * *

While that scene would be telecast on a particular channel and millions of eyes would be fixed on the figure emerging under the spotlight, another truth would unfold on a rival channel. It had to unravel parallel to that spectacle, thought the occupant of the Sumo Grande. The primetime news would feature a special investigative report on that musical bonanza and reveal the dark secrets of its local, nay, national star, the music maestro. A sensational revelation of deceit and plagiarism.

The young, energetic driver of the Sumo Grande was bursting with excitement. He was a veteran in investigative reporting and sting operations. Addicted to unearthing truths and breaking news, he was ambitious and knew that he was just inches away from the highest national award for young journalists and from the most exclusive professional circles.

Looking at his drowsy comrade, the cameraman, the driver of the Sumo Grande prayed that he hit the target tonight. He was ready to do anything. The song which began to play on the music system was the famous song of the maestro, 'The Primitive Prayer'.

This was the song which Momoko had given birth to on that night when the eyes of the tiger were burning and Cheng was howling under the sleep-deprived moon. The maestro had been nominated for the same song. It was the title track of the album which had reached the peak of popularity. The song had touched the hearts of music lovers and critics alike and gave a mythical touch to the maestro's iconic image. And it was also the song due to which the drivers of both the Ford Icon and the Sumo Grande were rushing towards two diametrically opposite tasks. They had forgone the lure of cosy air-conditioned bedrooms and were blinking excitedly, mentally revising the points and mouthing the dialogues.

They were like young interns preparing their first presentation before the panellists of an interview board.

Presentation is the key, the essence of everything. Presentation and packaging. Packaging of a person, packaging of an item, packaging of a tune and packaging of spirits. It is an art and a game. The bottom line is saleability in the market. Two experts in the art or the game were travelling to increase the saleability or to sustain the market value of their respective products and professions. Both were rehearsing the dialogues, the strategy to follow when presenting before the world the real composer of 'The Primitive Prayer', the song that made it as this year's chartbuster.

* * *

The original song, which pierced the frozen heart and oozed out of the salty lips of Momoko, had been displaced. It had crossed the hilly terrains and jungles to the world of metallic bling and tech-driven symphonies at the opposite pole of the world. In the process of migration, the song had undergone a makeover. Its tone and tenor, rhythm and heartbeat had changed. Its face had changed. It is said that a plain face sans makeup could look so beautiful, so alluring. So it was with the song.

A young geologist who had come in search of a megalith in one of the caves in the hills had stared with deep admiration at Momoko's face blessed with natural beauty. She was taking him and his team on a guided tour. By the time they returned, the sun was retreating. The members of the geology team were tired. They had sat down in the shadow of the sal trees which dotted the mouth of the caves.

Momoko, leaning on a huge stone, was looking at the sun that was turning a bright red. Its rays illuminated Momoko's face, making it look like a blood-red flower. The red flower was busy watching the retreating sun as it spread its colours in the sky. As she was watching the bright bamboos, which the innumerable rays of the sun had painted on the sky, the infant tied to her body started howling.

Thrusting the child to her bosom, she let him suck the nectar from her white spotless shellflower, singing the song, haltingly, hauntingly. It was an unfamiliar tune, like hundreds of mysterious insects chorusing a primitive prayer that resonated in the deep dark jungle. The tune had slipped from her salty lips like the appeal of a broken heart or a broken soul. The haunting tune had entangled itself with the fragrance of the evening. Like the waves of the ocean, the deep sound of the tune had submerged the forests, hills and the rocky caves.

That was the beginning ...

* * *

Yes, that was when the tune reached a curious human ear outside the hills for the first time. The young geologist searching for a megalith was the first to hear it. And it was he who, unknowingly, played his part in the migration of the ethnic song germinated in the ancient hills ...

That's how the story of the song began. It migrated to the city from the hills. The song, which was held captive in the tape recorder of the geologist, fell into the hands of a music lover. It changed hands over a few drinks and lay dormant in the personal archive of the music lover for a while. A few years later, the song was heard by an enthusiastic musicologist who retrieved it from the music lover's archive with care and included it in a music pool that was aptly titled 'The Tribal Oral Folk Song Tradition'. This was for a project called World Heritage, sponsored by the United Nations. As part of that priceless treasure trove, the song remained in hibernation for a few more years. One day, during a random browsing session by a research scholar, the song was woken from its slumber . . .

Oh, good lord! What a spell Momoko's melody had on the body and soul of that man! That night itself, after inhaling some intoxicating glue, he felt drawn to the song and held tight the hand of his musician friend. The two were high and felt swayed by the primitive tune. It took the form of a soothing lullaby and embraced them. The song reincarnated Momoko as if she were an ancient mother and they surrendered to her. They had never met her yet were so familiar. An unknown pain hit them. Paralyzed by that heart-wrenching pain, they got drawn into an ocean of sleep. They had never slept like that before. They slept a deep post-coital sleep, listening to the murmurs of the faraway hills, birds, wildflowers and the whispering tiger!

What a bright sunny morning it was the next day! The musician who had slept like a baby in the arms of his friend the previous night decided to offer the song to his guru. It would be a wonderful New Year's gift, he thought.

While Momoko was plucking the ripe golden corns in the faraway hills humming another lullaby, 'The Primitive Prayer' made it to a recording studio in the city. She had no idea that on the floor of the studio, her song was being given new layers and textures. Momoko's voice shrunk underneath the onslaught of instruments and digital mixes. Her voice, laced with the deep mystery of a wild insect, began losing direction.

Like a tiny bird dies after a thunderstorm and lies motionless at the foot of a tree, the soul of the song too died. Only its façade remained. For those who had given Momoko's song a makeover in the studio, it was just a rhythmic extravaganza. They didn't realize that a song could have a soul and heartbeat of its own. For them it was just a product, a commodity to be sold with good packaging.

'Do you want to go back to the past? Let's go. For the past is our future.' The back cover of the album boasted the lines, 'Music knows no man-made boundaries. To share and enjoy together, we are celebrating world music.' So there came the big event of releasing the new sensational song by them! The song was packaged in a colourful cover by a famous music label that camouflaged the fact that the song had travelled thousands of miles. The song finally hit the stores with a big bang. Soon millions were swaying their hands and heads to the wild, undulating tune.

* * *

'Yes, it is trending and is a chartbuster!' The driver of the Sumo Grande was reading the latest news from the music industry and was amazed that the song had crossed all previous record sales. He sensed the trickery in the statement made by the guru's recording banner that music has no boundaries. It was cleverly used to adapt Momoko's song without credit and call it their own. For instance, the music maestro had kept the first line in Momoko's native language and added a few of his own lines, which he thought were poignant, towards the end. If Momoko had mentioned a tiger and a caterpillar, the music guru changed it to moonlight and wildflower.

Meanwhile, a soft breeze filled with the fragrance of mustard flowers suddenly hit the driver of the Ford Icon and he inhaled deeply, enjoying the aroma after such a long time. But just then the car bumped into a boulder with such force that he almost fell out. Good lord! He had no clue that these bumpy country roads had such steep curves and boulders. He lit a cigarette and thought about Momoko again. He knew very well that Momoko, singing thousands of miles away in complete isolation of the hills where he was headed, had no clue what was going on.

How on earth was a simple woman like Momoko to know that transnational music companies, in the name of world heritage, were scouting for songs from the hills and jungles around the world, which they would later present to the multimillion-dollar global market?

The driver of the Ford Icon threw the cigarette packet out of the window. The packet got lodged in the thorny wild bushes across the road and stuck out like an ugly pimple on the face of the lush greenery around. Suddenly he noticed a Sumo Grande. In the rear-view mirror, he could see a wild boar running across.

As things stood, Momoko's song had been nominated for the highest musical award and a nosy journalist driving a Sumo Grande was on the verge of uncovering the truth. For him, the song was a sensational breaking story. The reverse journey to the origin of the song was underway. Looking for the epicentre of the song, tearing through the pitch darkness of the night, the drivers of the Sumo Grande and the Ford Icon rehearsed how they would approach the truth. One to create a sensation in the media and the other to buy out Momoko with a bribe or a false promise.

Rehearsing their respective parts, the drivers of the Ford Icon and Sumo Grande moved towards the focal point of the story of the displaced song. That's where Momoko was waiting.

* * *

Momoko was like a firefly. Living in nature's lap, her life was a simple one and so were her thoughts. Her wisdom came from the enlightening glow of a life lived amidst hills and thick jungles. Her grand truths were those obtained by living in the proximity of nature. Which is why when the face of a man mauled by a tiger dwelled on her subconsciousness, the Mukindan Hill, which the dead passed by on their final journey, recurred in her nightmares; when the ruthless deity, Cholera Devi, snuffed out the life of the child in her lap; and when Hung, Cheng's offspring, had howled like a jackal making an entry into the world, Momoko tirelessly kept singing.

She was the wife of a man who was killed by a tiger. In that part of the world nobody would shed a tear for someone dragged away by a tiger, for a tiger was believed to be a pure deity. One got shredded to pieces by a tiger because of bad karma. But how can one not cry for her partner? How can one's beloved be a sinner? That's why Momoko sang.

Expelling the thickened blood of her heart through her salty lips, Momoko kept singing. She infused the blood from her heart in the songs she had inherited from her elders and passed them on to the young and energetic boy, Hung, who was on his way to adulthood. She explained the meaning and significance of each song. The songs seeped into the core of his being. Sometimes with a flute and sometimes with the strings of a *sarinda*, he would bring them out. Even with the shiny instrument with a narrow waist, which he had brought from the city, he would hold it on a diagonal position in front of her, and play the lullaby inspired by the hudu bird, which she had sung to him. With the strings of the guitar, he could beautifully tie up her songs. Not just the sound of flute and sarinda, but also the melody of the guitar would reverberate in Momoko's wide courtyard.

* * *

Those who liked to visualize tribal belts as primitive areas frozen in the past for eternity would be shocked at the sound of the guitar in Momoko's courtyard. Standing there, the two visitors, who alighted from the Sumo Grande and Ford Icon, were in for a surprise. Getting lost, driving around on a curvaceous path, the Sumo Grande had suffered a punctured tyre. The journalist, exhausted after driving on that torturous road which could shake one up right from the extremities to each joint of the body, was changing the tyre and panting heavily when the Ford Icon reached the spot. Seeing the Ford Icon, the journalist was shocked. This was the protégé of the musical maestro! The suspicion of the journalist in the Sumo Grande came alive. The number one protégé of the guru coming to buy off the old woman to cover up the allegations would be proof of the great musical guru's act of plagiarism.

Looking at the condition of the Sumo Grande, the protégé in the Ford Icon smiled to himself. 'So, the news about this son of a gun doing a story against guru*ji* is confirmed now.' Thank god, he felt he could at least breathe easy knowing that 'the bastard' had not already negotiated with Momoko. There was no need for any pretence since everything was out in the open. It would be a face-to-face deal. He thought he would need to shut 'this flea's mouth' along with that of the old woman. It was a question of money. 'Can be done, but not without a good fight,' he said to himself.

With all kinds of permutations and combinations weighing on their minds, the drivers of the Ford Icon and Sumo Grande became tense. When both parties realized that it was time for a confrontation, they became like warring wild cats or leopards. Their eyes focused on the first sign of attack—who would make the first move. As the air between the two heated up, suddenly the melodious sound of a guitar came floating through the air.

From behind the ladder on the *changghar*, a face was looking at them with curiosity. Even though the face was covered with cobweb-like wrinkles, radiant with an inner glow, it reflected serenity and love—it was the face of Momoko!

Sitting on the bamboo floor of the changghar and sipping flavourful, cool liquor with chunks of roasted meat offered by Momoko, the two visitors, exhausted from long travel, felt rejuvenated. They felt like dropping to the floor and sleeping, forgetting all their worldly problems. The aim of their journey seemed utterly meaningless. What mattered was the delicate touch of the cool breeze, those two bowls of flavourful homemade rice beer and the face, chiselled by time, as it gazed at them with motherly affection.

Overpowered by enticing drowsiness, with a wobbly tongue, the young journalist asked Momoko, 'Who just played guitar here? I never thought in my dreams that I would hear the sound of guitar in this remote place.'

If the visitors were surprised to hear the guitar, they were all the more surprised to see the two young, well-built boys, who had come out responding to Momoko's call. One was attired in an oversized T-shirt and tight jeans and the other was completely punk—feather-cut hair, tattoos on the arms and a pair of low-slung striped trousers.

'Look at you two, you look so completely urbane,' the young journalist commented.

'Why? You expected us to come out naked or in our loin-cloth?'

Throwing a glance at the laughing face of her grandchild Hung, Momoko introduced the other boy, Hung's friend Chomang. As Chomang, who had been associated with a modelling agency and contemporary dance academy in a metropolitan city for several years, started talking about music bands and television channels and the media with the guests, the protégé said, 'Such a beautiful hilly place, fresh air, tranquil atmosphere, what a view—like an impressionist painting. It must be heavenly to live here.'

'It's nice—to sit idle and watch the hills, to write poetry—but when the malaria mosquitoes get you and you have to reach the government dispensary walking on this unnegotiable road for several hours, such visual aesthetics become useless,' Hung laughed out loud once more.

Hung's answer seemed to have jolted those two out of their romantic, luxurious mood. It was time for real-world issues, not for soul-searching in dreamy romanticism. Immediately, they both went back to their objective, which just moments ago had seemed petty, hollow and meaningless.

It was time to talk business. The friction in the air was palpable. The air was heating up with arguments and counterarguments and the sparks that flew from threats and counter threats. Momoko, with an expressionless face, listened to their business talk. No one could tell what was going on inside her head, whether she understood what was being said. The driver of the Sumo Grande asked Momoko to sing the song before the camera and goaded her to mention the geologist's name and all related events in detail. In a patronizing tone, he also asked her to condemn the act of the music guru, who was minting money and gaining worldwide fame with a stolen song. The driver of the Ford Icon appealed to Momoko in an intimidating tone to let go of the past and settle for repayment in cash or kind. He also promised her that in the second edition, her name would be included in the album. Moreover, an album containing all the lullabies, the songs of love and death and hymns sung by Momoko would be brought out by them and Momoko would be famous. The battle of words by two men centering on Momoko went on till the late afternoon. Looking at the statuesque Momoko amidst the whirlpool of arguments–counterarguments, Chomang whispered into Hung's ears, 'Look at what our old woman is made of, she comes from the Stone Age, our *satjug*. If she only gives her bytes, she will be famous overnight. Each channel will come running to take her footage, she will be loaded with what they will pay—look at how desperate both the parties are—she will get as much as she wants.'

'I will get as much as I want,' Momoko startled everyone by speaking suddenly. Her eyes strayed over the blue-grey hills and soaked in the unparalleled beauty of the sky, and she spoke, as if in a trance, 'Nature will give me as many songs as I want. The crickets will give them, that air zooming like an arrow through the trees will give them, the toads and frogs will give them—there is no dearth of songs for me here. As there is no shortage of songs, what would I do with your money? You people are needy. I don't need money, but you do, to buy songs. You need money to buy songs . . .'

Taking her eyes off the protégé who came in the Ford Icon, she turned towards the journalist who had come in the Sumo Grande, 'I am not going to sing standing in front of your picture-machine, please don't mind. If someone is singing my song as his own, let him sing. He is doing this because he is poor. I have donated my song to him. I sing when I want to sing and if some soul desires to listen to my song, he or she can. Songs are divine souls. They should not be traded. I cannot sell such pure souls out of greed. Who can steal our songs, even if the entire world tries? If someone lays claim on our songs, would our songs cease to be ours?'

Amused, Momoko started laughing. The two men by then wore the expression of two foolish boys caught stealing by their mother, and Momoko laughed loudly. Adding shine and colour to her laughter, the sky took on the hue of bright red. The sun was about to set on the horizon. Like a mother who shows the infant on her lap a rainbow in the sky, Momoko drew their attention to the sky and said, 'Look, what do you see—can you see the sun stretching its thousand bright rays, the *Ra-bah*? Can you all see the dazzle of the Ra-bah? Do you know how long their brightness lasts? Just for a few moments. The moment the sun sets, everything is over. The end of Ra-bah's brightness, the end of momentary glory; after that there is nothing but darkness.'

As the valley drowned in darkness and the sun bade a final goodbye, the crickets started singing. A barred owl hooted in the wood. No, it was a mourning dove chanting. In a nearby pond, the green toad leapt up to the sky and sang a hymn. The wind whistled through the bamboos. Momoko started humming 'The Primitive Prayer'. Drenched in this blended melody of an ethereal chorus, these two men from the faraway metropolitan city sat stupefied looking at this woman called Momoko, the Stone Age woman.

Andhika Parv

Dedicated to Baby Haldar and Lakshmi Urang

'Gabhisti! Gabhisti!'

Who had uttered those words?

Those were not words but arrows stained with the venom of a poisonous snake, hitting my mind, the bloodstream transmitting the news of death to every pore of my body. In the din of festivities and the chanting of mantras by 2000 pious priests, how could this arrow of words hit me?

'Seva, Seva—Sevu, Sevu.'

Another equally deadly arrow of words hit me. As one poison neutralized the effect of another, that shot jolted me from the hazy world of thoughts and memories, and I fell on the floor. The angry, authoritarian shout from Rajlakshmi. If I were late in my response even by a moment, instead of calling me Seva, she would use the name the naughty children in the palace used for me—'Sevu, Sevu.' I had allowed myself the luxury of roaming into the world of thoughts and memories momentarily, and I was done.

Human beings need time for reminiscing. Agnidev, are we free even for a moment? We are solely responsible for keeping you burning in the hearth of each master's house. Like your blazing inferno, the fire that lights up with discipline and diligence in our hearts, too, is inextinguishable. The moment an opportunity presents itself, our tired body passes out in no time. Like a horse, it naps standing on its legs. When it finally hits the sack, within seconds it turns into a stony slab—stiff, motionless. Still, like the rainwater seeping through the impenetrable foliage in a dense jungle, the droplets of our thoughts seep into our consciousness through those never-ending chores and drench us. We too are seeds of humans. We too have a mind and a soul, and the ability to think.

Ignorantly, the masters think that we are beyond such capacity. We are inanimate objects; our minds are devoid of the ripples of thoughts. We are lowly animals, we just know how to bray and gesticulate to express our needs like hunger, thirst and sex.

That day, in the pleasure house, the Rangashaala, there were rehearsals for the Vasant Utsav. A play, based on the love story of an apsara and a king, was to be staged. Carrying tasty food and somras for the actors, I watched a scene in which the king and his slave were having a conversation. The royal one was speaking in a cultured tone and with standard diction, but his servitor was incomprehensible with uncouth words.

With spit spilling over a mouth chewing betel nut and paan, he spoke making strange gestures and wore the distorted body language of a clown. I understand that jesters are important for the sake of entertainment, but in this entire world is there not a servitor who is calm, quiet, intelligent and a pleasant talker? After giving our days and nights to cater to the needs of those to whom we have given our body and mind—co-existing, cohabiting—won't their language germinate its roots and grow on our tongues too?

The language I had inherited from my parents was a different one. During the journey from that house to the abode of the royal blacksmith, the high-profile merchant and finally to this royal palace, have I not learnt to speak this classical language fluently? Have I ever been credited for this?

Rajlakshmi never tells me, 'Go, dear Seva. Complete your work fast,' whereas she addresses the cattle and other animals with such warmth and softness, 'Come Gaumata, come. Honour us with your milk and curd.' We are treated like a bunch of disobedient, unruly monkeys. She uses the same harsh tone for us as she would to shoo them away, 'Go, go, Sevu. Hurry up. Work, work.' Work that's endless, immense, and mountain-like.

You know Agnidev, we are not afraid of work. Our work is tougher than grazing the cattle or farming, but if there is an umbrella of the blue sky over the head, the body is caressed by the damp breeze carrying the fragrance of the season, and the feet are licked by the soft green tongue of the earth, that's not called work. Standing in this suffocating kitchen, sizzling with heat, smoke and fire, amidst those rows of cooking vessels, when our arms turn raw stirring the boiling content in these huge pans with ladles, who would know our pain better than you? The bowls of spices which we grind in that stone mortar? The concentration it requires to get the blend right. If the ingredients are not mixed in the right proportion, the mixture will lose its characteristic properties. The taste of the cuisine will change and there will be a breakdown in the household. What can one say about the fragrant body packs that we prepare for the women of the royal family. Even the ghee, oil, curd and butter needed for the consumption of the royal household must be churned by us. Someone from the enemy kingdom might poison the food if it is brought from outside.

When the time comes for the ceremonial initiation of the royal princesses into studying the sixty-four arts, we have to get everything together, starting with the rangoli making. We have to prepare red colour from red stones, yellow from cow urine, collect thousands of flowers for flower decorations, supply them with everything required for jewellery design, perfume making, needles and threads for embroidery and whatnot. The work is endless and immense.

In the dead of the night, when the mating call of a deer comes floating from the jungle, when the sad calls of separated chakoi-chakua birds fill the air at regular intervals, when the world goes to sleep, submerged in a melancholic calm, we have to cater to the needs of our gods.

The night duties are the most difficult and painful, O Agnidev.

Taking turns, we go to the bedrooms of royalty, or to the pleasure houses, carrying vessels of liquor and fragrant massage oil. Their lust and aggression turn into thousands of wagging tongues and lick us all over.

Like worker bees hovering day and night over the beehives on the branches of tall trees, we work round the clock. With faces silent and expressionless, we keep buzzing around the hive-like palace, every day, day and night, and when there are festivities and guests from far-flung areas—kings and Brahmins—pouring into the palace in hordes, then us bees create a storm, turn into battle horses, and, cracking the whip on us, the riders scream, 'Work, work, hurry, hurry.'

Today is the day of a big festival. The air is resonating with the unforgettable chorus of 2000 pious priests reciting mantras. The air is filled with the fragrance of pitchers of ghee burning in the holy fire, and of scented flowers. Pausing for a moment, I see, to my utter surprise, like white foam or ivory, there is a milk-white royal horse. Brahmins and the royal princes are bathing him with divine water carried in hundreds of gold pitchers. Applying fragrance and adorning him with marvellous cloth and ornate jewellery. Offering flowers at his feet, they are putting a gold chain around his neck and bringing him to the *yagyakhestra*. In that *yagyakunda*, the head priest and the 2000 pious Brahmins chanting the mantra are getting ready for the Purna.

The face of Draupadi amidst her five husbands emerges in the golden flame of the sacrificial fire. Mesmerized, I look at the radiant face of the dusky woman. This face has turned black like a buffalo. A menstruating woman covered in a single piece of cloth was being dragged to the packed royal court. As if a hundred and one poisonous arrows had pierced her soul.

The same way the poisonous arrow of words hit my mind. Cutting across the thick layer of the chants made by thousands of pious ones, it hit my senses. Whenever I hear this word, my soul, my body freezes. Gabhisti, Gabhisti.

Isn't the Ashwamedha Yagya a bigger form of Gabhisti? If Gabhisti is an armed campaign in search of Gowdhan, then Ashwamedha Yagya, too, is a similar armed campaign for annexing new territories. Sometimes in the name of cows, sometimes in the name of territory, armed campaigns, battles, bloodshed. How many battles have I seen, how many have I heard of, how many more to come?

* * *

That was a night from our adolescent years. Having completed the meal, sitting around the fire lit on the floor, the elderly men of the family were chewing fragrant betel-nut and discussing something important. Our mother and a few other women were stitching *godhas* with big needles. A godha is a bracelet made of deer skin which one wears on the left hand to protect it from getting hurt during archery. The spine-chilling neighing of thousands of horses blended with the sound of their hoofs. Hiding behind the bushes of one of the hillocks in our village, in terror and breathless bewilderment, I saw, brighter than the stars, countless twinkling lights moving in a long procession, rushing by the foothills. Their movement was making a howling sound, like the sound that precedes a terrible thunderstorm. What a terrifying scene. Pressing my chest, my mother whispering, 'Gabhisti. That's a Gabhisti raid. Those armed riders must be the soldiers of the new kingdom.'

Raising our fear and destroying our paddy fields, that team of riders zoomed off towards the hills in the north. Gowdhan and horse—empowered by these two blessed animals, the powerful new kingdom was steadily growing in this part of the land.

Ours was a cluster of twenty odd villages of the Das tribe. The head of our village was my grandfather. Wise villagers would gather around the fire and my grandfather to discuss everything, besides debating political issues, going through the farming accounts, making of weapons or the ways to rear cattle; analysing problems related to health and other important issues, they used to keep themselves updated about the movements of the other ethnic groups in the vicinity.

Though the other children used to drift into sleep, I used to stay awake, listening to the conversations in rapt attention. There were terrifying stories of battles and clashes among ethnic groups. Grandfather would narrate, 'Travelling from faraway places, crossing thousands of mountains and canyons, the mighty conquerors were advancing towards this vast expanse of green land, which was the home for races like Gond, Naag, Sud, Paani, Bratya, Asur and our Das. Among all those warring ethnic groups, the Paani and Das were the strongest tribes.'

The stories of the Paani tribe were full of adventures. Tales of daring robberies by aggressive tribesmen had travelled wide and far. I used to fantasize that when I grew up, I would offer my love to the most intelligent, adventurous and dreaded thief from the Paani tribe. The people of our Das tribe were hardworking and peace-loving. Enriched with a huge cattle stock and endless stretches of undulating golden green paddy fields, we soared high like eagles. We had a wealthy archive of folktales, riddles and parables full of wisdom and knowledge handed down over generations. We had stories about everything in the universe to be narrated ritualistically every night around that fire. The scene we had witnessed on the night of the Gabhisti campaign, however, did not end just as a story.

Grandfather, father and others went silent and remained stupefied for a long time. Their faces had turned ashen like the skin of a wild buffalo in anticipation of some unforeseen threat. The mighty conquerors were marching forward like the monsoon flood, spreading their territory, and along with it, their enmity towards us.

There were differences in lifestyle, physical appearance, language, beliefs and customs. They who had always looked down upon us and described us thus in public gatherings, on the streets or in their epics, had adopted much of our wisdom, our knowledge, ways of working and even words from our language. They claimed them as their original creations. The lion's share of their knowledge of medicinal herbs came from the Das community's painstaking observations of their surroundings for generations. The knowledge of this land, of its forest, trees, creepers and bushes, flowers and seeds are on our fingertips. Our fathers and forefathers have been studying the medicinal properties of roots, leaves, flowers, insects and different muds since ancient times. That science was now given new nomenclature by the powerful ones. It all comes down to power, the ultimate truth. Whoever has power and supremacy controls religion, politics, epics, poetry and history. They become the sole bearers of knowledge, and culture.

The anxiety of an impending catastrophe reflecting on our fathers' and grandfathers' faces that night was not baseless. Once, when the evening deity was about to descend and our Gowdhan was about to return, our Mrigahasti team had returned in tatters. The leader of the team and the main mahout were missing. The conquerors were curious about the Mrigahasti. They had termed this huge, sober animal with a trunk a deer with one hand. Hence the name, Mrigahasti. Our people were experienced with domesticating and controlling elephants.

The herd of Mrigahasti of our village was lured out of the jungle and domesticated by grandfather and father and the other men in the village by chanting magic mantras. When the herd came back, running helter-skelter, everyone panicked. My grandfather was overcome with grief. A day later, on the banks of a torrential stream, the mutilated body of the mahout was found by some cowherds. A few days after that, slicing the darkness in the night, hundreds of dots of lights came towards us with the speed of an arrow, the air resonated with spine-chilling neighing of battle-crazed horses.

Everything changed after that. All the daughters of the village heads of the Das tribe became slaves in the households of the conquerors. Bodies covered with raw wounds, blood and pus oozing out of them, the legs and feet swollen, limping with elephantine legs, we walked miles and miles, broken and exhausted. Marching ahead of us were the cattle and Mrigahasti herds, carrying huge loads of clothes, jewellery, metal vessels and fighting tools, and at the end were the young men, women and children. The old and sick ones were killed. Some ran away. We, the prisoners of war, walked towards a life of slavery at the hands of our conquerors. Pillaging our hard work and self-respect, they became rich and powerful, and a new word was added to their vocabulary—Das. An independent indigenous ethnic group was removed from the pages of history and reduced to one word synonymous with a life of unpaid slavery.

I, Nidalu's daughter Savaya, Seva, became Sevu slave. The first address in the chain of my lifecycle as a slave was that of the royal blacksmith, Devdutta. He was an influential person in the town, a skilled chariot maker. The king, ministers, generals, soldiers, everyone used to get their chariots made by him. He was not a mere chariot maker. He was also a multitalented blacksmith, with a huge smithy.

Every day hundreds of iron ploughs were given shape in that inferno, and, like the blazing fire of the smithy, our pain too was red hot and self-consuming. Like the swollen hot iron ploughs, a different kind of swollen plough was ready to till the fertile ground of my adolescent body. Especially by the strong young man who was engaged in bringing firewood from the jungle to the smithy. He used to hide himself in the darkness, ready to pounce on me at the first chance.

Our employer was old, he was uninterested and virtuous, but he was not a saviour. If a maid got pregnant, it was a blessing for the employer. Like the Gowdhan, Dasdhan too flourished. By god's grace, I found salvation, sometimes because of some disease which was a blessing in disguise and saved me from some torturous nights and sometimes by the secret medicine of an old woman. I was certain that soon my life as a maid would come to an end and I would be reunited with my cowherd sculptor and be impregnated only by my lover and then live a blissful domestic life as his beloved wife.

The dream, still alive in some corner of my heart, helped me carry on through the darkest of days. I was moving step by step, but soon I came across a bottomless pit. The sway of my blossoming breasts enticed a respected nobleman, and, paying a hundred gold coins, that rich merchant took me away from the royal blacksmith to his den like a prized possession. After feasting on me for a few seasons, he then took me, the beautiful and perfect Sevudasi, as a gift to the royal palace of Hastinapur.

The day I had set foot on the grounds of this palace, the air was filled with festive fervour. The Rajsuya Yajna was going on. Kings, princes, godmen, *sanyasis* and the learned ones had come from far off places to participate in it. Rich merchants and businesspeople had contributed to this yajna with money and domestic help to work for that grand gala. The merchants always maintained cordial relations with the king. The blessings of the royals were important to rise in business, and contributions from this section of people were equally important to carry on with royal duties. From the merchant's side, I was taken to a special room. In that room, an elderly lady sitting on a decorated golden bed assessed me from head to toe. I felt like cattle or a horse up for sale. That elderly woman ordered her old maid, 'She is physically fit. Engage her in taking care of the guests.'

That night the responsibility that fell on me in the guest quarters was to take care of a wise old sage. In the flickering light of an earthen lamp, I saw him meditating on a *kushasan*. Bowing down in reverence to touch the feet of the mendicant with matted hair, I noticed his skin was dry and his heels were cracked like a parched field.

There was a stink coming from his feet, and I saw a patch of unsightly ringworm. The women of the royal family had taken over the duty of taking care of the important guests. We were to take care of their assistants. My share was this ringworm-ridden stinking sage. I felt nauseated. To top it off, I had witnessed a scene behind the living quarters of the *dasis*, where the cattle shed of the royal palace was located. A bull was kept there to supply divine meat for the feast. To feed the Gowdhan, they were preparing a special feed of millet and, nearby, the slaves were killing uncountable buffaloes, deer and goats. The stink of raw blood had filled the air and the solidified blood had taken the shape of a dome. There were stray dogs and crows circling above. Shaking me out of my thoughts, the carrier of the ringworm let me know that he was fasting. Relieved, as I was retreating, he uttered in his incoherent voice, 'The body of this dasi is fit for the ritual of Aghorpanthi Bamachar ...'

A chill passed through my body. I could be the Dyutiyogini for Bamachari meditation. I was aware that the other learned lot looked down upon the Bamachari practitioners, who regard the human body as the sacred site for Mahajajna where liquor, meat and copulation are offered as divine offerings by the inhabitants of crematoriums. I felt a surge of immense delight imagining that during that ritual, I too would be worshipped, even if just for a night. Each part of my naked body would be inhabited by some god and goddesses and the part where my thighs meet would be the *agnikund* of the Mahajajna, the sacred opening of divine fire where this devotee would offer his virility to attain salvation. It may be an illusion, but just for one night, I thought I would be free and independent. A life which was spent at the feet of everyone would now have someone at its feet. All these years, I had been silently but desperately waiting for some intelligent, philosophical, dagger-sharp debater from the Charuvak school, who would show the nullifying thumb to the functioning and customs of powerful masters and laugh in their face, but that night the burning desire to spend a night with an *aghori*, the mysterious creature of the crematorium, took root in my mind. As if bitten by a mad dog of insatiable desire, my body became effervescent, amorous and uncontainable.

That night, as I emerged from the guest quarters, I saw the outside world was flooded with moonlight. The full moon was shining in the sky, nostrils were filled with a sweet subtle fragrance and the body was caressed by a gentle breeze. On the way from the guest quarters to the living area of the dasis, there was a royal garden which was in full bloom.

Beneath one of the trees, two figures, a man and woman, were engrossed in intimate conversation. Who could be out at such late hours? The man was well-built, like a male elephant in its prime. His muscular torso was covered in a yellow cloth and his headgear had a peacock feather. He was the hero of numerous mythological dramas. Despite being an ordinary cowherd, with intelligence and political acumen, he had established the huge Yadav empire. Chandradev poured a fistful of white moonlight into my conscience. That mythical man stood before me. I felt an irresistible attraction towards him. In him I was searching for my lover, comparing their looks, praying that like this man, my beloved, too, becomes a dream lover.

Who was this dark woman with him, whose radiant beauty looked as if the sun god had focused all his rays to illuminate her?

Shyama padmapalashakshineel kunchitmurdhaja
Tam rtung nakhisubhrush charu pinapayodhara
Kamyam hi rupam Panchalya vidhatravihitam svayam
Babhuvadhi kamanya abhyah sarbhuta manoharam
Tesham tu Draupadim drishtva Sarveshamamitojasam
Sampramathaye indriya gramam praduraseen manobhavah.

They were Krishna and Draupadi aka Jagyaseni. The centre of attraction and curiosity. Her life was different from that of other women. Like many male goats copulated with a single female goat, she too was the single wife for all five husbands and the great Lord Krishna's bosom friend. They were relaxing under the ashoka tree pondering over the thoughts and emotions of this universe. She was free, wise, generous and self-aware. Despite being cultured, calm and all virtuous, she was considered proud.

We had heard that she had insulted Karna in front of the entire gathering in the Swayamvar because he was the son of a low-born chariot driver, Adhirath. How humiliated Karna must have felt, no one could know that better than me. While coming to take part in the Rajsuya Yajna, when Duryodhan was out of his depth because of the illusions cast by the architectural marvel of Mai Danav, she had laughed sarcastically. This proud looking, self-engrossed Draupadi had another side. Even with the company of five amazing men as husbands, she felt lonely. She was like a lake; nobody had a clue what lay at the bottom.

Only Krishna could create ripples in that deep, calm, ocean-like mind. Like the night mist infuses life into a night queen flower, Jagyaseni too becomes lively in his presence. Krishna was her truest friend forever.

I remembered the carefree adolescent days I had spent in the company of the cowherd sculptor. Our tribe had a ritual of worshipping our ploughs a day before we start ploughing our fields. We paid obeisance to the trees, the rocks and to mother earth. At night, as soon as the moon god made his appearance, a special ceremony for fertility began. First, the worshipping of the plough, and then all the girls of the village who had attained puberty would carry a branch of a tree covered with leaves and flowers, and, stark naked, they would encircle the entire field, singing and dancing and embracing the divine trees. The head priestess of this ritual, the elderly guru mother, had taught us the secret mantra for this ceremony, the ultimate truth of nature, that women and the earth shared a secret bond. We knew that only with the touch of a woman, the earth turns green, and trees bear flowers. Similarly, by drinking the juice of the trees, eating leaves and seeds and fruits and touching the roots, a woman became fertile.

How mysterious was the relationship between a tree and a woman? Like the ashoka flowers, they blossom only when the tree comes in touch with a woman's feet. Keshar, bakul, madhavi blossom with the liquid touch of a woman's saliva, the neem and mango trees are fruit-laden when they hear a woman's laughter. Karnikars are proud trees. Only when a woman speaks to them, their male stamens become erect. Nameru, tilak, rudraksha and the yellow flowers of kumkum blossom hearing a woman singing. Kadam and champak await the gentle touch of a woman to flower, and the stubborn, huge sidhabak tree! Only when a woman embraces it intimately and requests it to flower, do its stamens swell up. Gurumata, the head priestess, had shared many secret truths and wisdoms that night.

The main part of the custom took place in the middle of the field. In the moonlit night, dancing to the blessed and melodious music, an untouched maiden became one with the plough following the rhythm of the music. Riding it, she invoked the goddess of fertility and, in a trance, as the rhythm of the dance reached its climax, she became the goddess herself. I, too, had become the goddess for a night.

After the plough ceremony, while going to the river for a bath, I had seen a figurine of a woman carved out of stone. Sculpted on a rock by the road, the figure had wrapped one of her legs around a tree. Her raised arm was holding a branch with leaves and flowers. Intricately carved jewellery adorned her hair, neck and waist. The face of that nude woman resembled mine. Standing close to that slab of stone was a young man. He had a hammer and a chisel in his hands and his face was downcast in hesitation. This was the cowherd who comes from the village across that hill to graze his cattle in the grassland by the river. How did he sculpt this figurine? Had he witnessed the ceremony, which was forbidden for men to watch?

That was the first time I had come face to face with that cowherd sculptor. The last time I saw him was the night of the new moon when the Gabhisti had happened. The eastern sky was getting brighter. Amidst the devastation, the procession of prisoners of battle had already started. As I was being dragged by the horsemen, I saw him with eyes full of shock and tears, like a lovelorn elephant running after our horses, and then an arrow went through his left arm at lightning speed. His heartrending scream and dilated eyes followed me through that journey.

I wondered if I would ever see him in this lifetime? Would I ever go back to the place of my childhood? With the decayed bodies of my father, mother, friends scattered on the land, would golden jwar ever be sown there? Would I ever find that nude sculpture in the deep jungle, near that cascading river? That blue sky, the rows of gambharika and sidhabak trees, the soft creamy touch of the tongue of the cowherd on the lips, that sensual dance, the taste of the honey-coated buffalo meat roasted in fire, and the intricately designed cool floor of hay of the bamboo and woodhouse where I would sleep on summer nights?

In contrast, here I was in my dark, dingy room. Where did the sleep in my eyes go? Did I leave it behind on that cool floor on the night of Gabhisti? Who will bring my sleep back and those soft, colourful dreams? In the dingy room, my eyes stay wide open, my hands become rough with grinding spices, and the ploughed, exhausted body a ground for cruel assault by uncountable buffaloes. The body which once used to be a source of pleasure has now become the arena for insults and torment.

* * *

The woman's body is a piece of land. Unleashing aggression, one must lay claim on it. Why does a woman's body become the destination for all injustice, insults, disgrace? Even after defeating a competitor, why is the body of the woman close to him targeted? Power and possession are the ultimate rule. Possessing a body conveys that I have power and ownership over all your properties. Who would teach these fools called men that laying claim over a heart is much higher than laying claim over a body? There is the tendency of disrobing a woman. In the process of disrobing lies the satisfaction of one's ego rather than lustful desire—a morbid, limitless gratification of one's pride that stems from showing off power and ownership. It is not the disrobed body which excites and satisfies the men, as much the process itself which exudes power and fills them with the feeling of machismo. Egos are satisfied at the expense of a naked body. What kind of a weak, amoral, spineless soul does one have to be? My experiences as a slave, a bonded worker, have made me realize these truths. Had I been born a subjugated slave, I would not have felt so bitter, accepting it as my destiny. But how can someone who has tasted freedom accept the bondage of slavery? Only the one who has seen daylight can realize how thick the darkness of the night is. Has anyone experienced a destiny opposite of mine?

Jagyaseni had experienced that irony. That is why I feel a connection with her. Jagyaseni Draupadi had known how insulting and unbearable it is to be disrobed forcefully. Right in front of her relatives, friends, the public and, closest of the close, her five husbands in a royal court. This incident was unprecedented in history. The scene comes before my eyes—a menstruating Draupadi in a single piece of cloth being dragged by her hair by Dushashan to the courtroom ...

Tato Dushasanorajan Draupdya Vasanambalat
Sabha Madhya samakshipya vyapabrishum
Akrishymane vasane Draupdyshchintitoharih

I feel her helplessness in my bones. The distress and suffering assume the shape of a huge python and gobbles me up slowly, steadily, and my entire entity has been plunged into an ocean of darkness. I heard that during the exile, while crossing many miles, Draupadi and her five husbands had reached the kingdom of a barbarian tribe. Their soldiers had attacked and injured Panchpandav fatally. In the deep, dense jungle, the unconscious Panchpandav and one unarmed, lonely, helpless woman. The unimaginable happened. Draupadi, it is said, roaring like a wild lioness, had picked up the bow of Arjun.

Where was that valiant avatar of Draupadi hiding during her *chirharan*? Why didn't she take the bow from Arjun and hit Duryodhan and Dushasan with arrows? Perhaps she was feeling weak that time with the menstrual bleeding. But the real reason was that Draupadi was emotionally weak. A weakness that stemmed from the trust in her own people. Her faith and dependence on her five husbands and relatives made her weak. When a person knows that they are all by themselves, they cannot depend on anyone, cannot trust anyone, then she or he faces this ultimate truth that you are on your own, and becomes invincible. The moment people realize that there is nothing to lose, they face life head on. The way Draupadi had picked up Arjun's bow that day and the way my cowherd sculptor revealed his secret facing hundreds of enemies with nothing but a mutilated body.

The day I had arrived in the royal palace there was a Rajsuya Yajna taking place. After that, when the invitees started to leave the palace one by one, suddenly I came face to face with a youth. He was the younger brother of my lover, my cowherd sculptor. Those days, how we played, roamed around the jungle together to pick up edible roots, to catch squirrels and mynahs with this young man. My body trembled with both trepidation and joy. He came as a caretaker of the horse of a king from a faraway kingdom. In the pretext of offering him betel-nut and paan, I called him closer and planned to meet at midnight in one of the corners of the garden.

Even though he was injured by an arrow during that Gabhisti night, my lover had managed to escape his village along with a few others. Among them was this younger brother of his. The paddy fields were destroyed. The entire cattle stock was looted. Travelling across hills and valleys on foot for several days, they had reached another kingdom. Trying to make a living by selling small toys and vessels made of clay and stone on the streets of that town, they were noticed by a generous artist. He took them both to his workshop. Familiar with the ways of the mighty conquerors, their lifestyle and language, they could pass off as one of them. They arrived at the huge workshop of the artist. There was the constant sound of the hammer and chisel. The younger one learnt the process of metal casting and the cowherd sculptor's drawing and engraving skills left everyone mesmerized. Was Mai Danav's blood running in the veins of his body? His reputation spread not just within the kingdom but the entire region. Orders for new and innovative works started pouring in and, between the two workshops in the town, this one became more popular.

After working the entire day in the workshop, all the workers and artists used to go to public places or some place of entertainment for a game of dice. With his sad eyes that cowherd was always in a different world. A curious mind in the pursuit of creativity. The sound of the hammer would come out of his studio even at night. One day everyone could see the stone figure he had been working on. How could a hard medium like stone exude so much softness, so much emotion, such allure? Nobody could recall seeing such beauty personified in an inanimate figurine. A nude woman, wavy hair, smooth neck and a tiny waist adorned with intricately designed jewellery. Full, mature, bell fruit-like breasts. The gold girdles betraying a hint of a rounded mound. The nude figure, which had all the aesthetics described in the *shilpashastra*, was standing in a triangular posture, with one of her legs wrapped around a tree. Her raised arm was holding a branch of a tree covered with leaves and flowers. The sculptor informed everyone, 'She is a celestial being, the goddess of fertility. I have seen this goddess dancing in the field on a moonlit night with my own eyes. It could be a divine encounter or a dreamlike, magical reality—a supernatural illusion. She is real, she is my goddess of fertility, whom I saw once dancing with a branch of agambharika tree on a full moon night.' His statement created a furore in the land. The idol was established in the sanctum sanctorum of the newly constructed temple. One day when with dance, music and offerings, with fervour and festivity, that nude figure was being carried in a long procession of devotees to the temple, a mysterious smile touched the lips of the sculptor. Everyone was singing his praise.

The path of intellect and talent is not an easy one, Agnidev. Its destiny is a thorny path full of jealousy and arrogance. If one is gifted, then mediocre rivals make that thorny path bloodier. There begins a campaign to eliminate that talent. Especially if that talent belongs to the powerless and the poor from the underprivileged class. Acknowledgement of talent, too, is dependent on social divides, Agnidev. In a land where the thumb was demanded as *gurudakshina* from tribesman Ekalavya, you can well fathom the situation. The agony of that mental warfare is no less than any Gabhisti, O Agnidev!

This exactly is what happened to my lover. The artists of the rival workshops and his co-artists ganged up to lay thorns in his path. Somehow, a couple of them dug out the truth that he was a migrant from a different kingdom, a man from the Das tribe. A conspiracy came into play. He was pronounced guilty of pilfering gold from the workshop, which was meant for making idols in the royal palace. According to the justice system of the mighty conquerors, a man pronounced guilty had to prove his innocence by touching a red-hot iron axe with his tongue. For my sculptor, along with his tongue, his hands too were ordered to touch the axe. When his burnt tongue and both hands failed to prove his innocence, his punishment was decided—pay twenty cattle and gold coins or leave town. How could an ordinary artist working in a workshop pay that much, Agnidev? Everyone in the market wanted to be free of competition, free of that inimitable and incomparable artistic persona.

After lashing him with a cane and iron chains, as the soldiers were about to drag him onto the highway to shunt him out of town, my lover with great difficulty muttered out the great secret. He said it in front of a few prominent people of the kingdom—the group of competitors, the priest of the royal temple and the members of the court of justice. Like the unarmed Draupadi, in the twilight moment of life and death all fears, all hesitation evaporated. With the bow of truth, my lover defeated the barbarian gathering of injustice. With a burnt tongue, he laughed out loud, 'Just because I am a lowly Das, all my honesty and talent have become meaningless? You all throw me out, but what will you do with that idol? She is the goddess of fertility, but she became a goddess only for a night. She, too, is a Das like me. An ordinary woman, and to tell the truth, this meeting, too, was not a divine phenomenon. Only my love turned it divine because she was my first and only love. My love is divine. That's why I am not afraid at all now. Even now I can smell the fragrance of that divine flower. Ah, such intoxicating fragrance!'

Everyone was stunned at the dangerous revelation. On first impulse they decided to inform everyone about the truth, but on second thoughts, they decided to bury it. It would have been a shameful admission. To destroy the idol, they would have to destroy parts of the temple and that would be a bad omen. Besides, in the time of drought, contributions for the reconstruction of the temple would be an added burden on the citizens. It was decided to purify that nude figure with their ritual of bathing the idol with milk and holy water and upgrade her to the status of a goddess. It was also decided that she would not be given the prime pedestal in the middle of the sacred temple space but in the gateway pillars or some niche in the wall.

Since then, my lover disappeared. He was nowhere to be seen, no village, no jungle, no settlement, nowhere. Like the bubbles merge in the water and smoke fuses into the air, he just vanished into the darkness of that evening. The way he was displaced from his hills once by Gabhisti, he was again displaced from this world, from life itself, so that he could not reveal the secret once again.

In the name of keeping the reputation of the race and in the name of removing a blot from history, he was sacrificed. The root cause of all these misdoings was that special equation—the equation between power and the desire to secure monopoly in a competitive market. The equation of power and wealth. My lover must have read that equation clearly. That's why he became indomitable—not caring for anything, strong because he had the truth by his side and ultimately came out triumphant. Everyone saw his mutilated body being dragged towards the border, but nobody saw that the path he was dragged onto culminated in a cascading river. There was a huge playground by the river, where a fierce competition of chariot racing had taken place that day among the princes and upperclassmen. Who keeps count of all those who are crushed under the wheels of the chariots and the hoof of the horses? Those numbers that remained outside the counting were washed away into another frontier of nothingness in the torrid current of a gushing river.

That night, in an obscure corner of the royal garden, when it was time for the stars to extinguish their fire, one by one, they climbed down to offer their fire to my heart. I was made to carry the fire of uncountable stars in my heart forever. In the heat of that fire my entire body was damp with sweat and my childhood friend, the younger brother of my beloved, with great affection took off the scarf from his shoulders and silently kept wiping off the sweat from my forehead and the tears from my eyes. The sound of the chariot wheels and the hooves of horses hit my ears.

Those guests who were left behind had started on their return journey. The sound of all the horses seemed to have become the battle cry and created tremors in my angered blood. I knew those tottering horses in my blood would never initiate a Dharmayudha, the way insult and anger in Draupadi had started one. A war where bloodshed had flooded the earth and the air, and the stink of hundreds of decaying corpses had suffocated even the vultures. A war like that would never start for me, for some woman like me, a woman who is a dasi, a maidservant, a slave-woman of lower birth and class. To start a Dharmayudha like that, no Krishna has been born in this world till date.

* * *

Lord Krishna is playing the *sankh* as a symbol of the successful ending of the Ashwamedh Yajna. At the end of Dharmayudha, there was another campaign to conquer the world. Another Gabhisti. Once again, the chariot wheels had started spinning. Another stream of blood flowed. In the wheels of history, there are bloodstains. The noise of festivity was evident all around—dance, music, songs. Forgetting the insult of her disrobing, there was Draupadi, radiant with the win of the Dharmadyudha and success of the Ashwamedha Yajna, smiling sweetly as she enjoyed the sound of the victory *sankh* blown by Lord Krishna. Her smile is that of a proud woman, and the words ring in my ears.

'Sevu, Sevu, work, work,
Hurry, hurry, hurry.'
Endless, never ending, mountain-like tasks.

The *chirharan* of Draupadi, her disgraceful disrobing, has ended. But not mine. Soon I will have to be ready with the pots of somras and massage oil. And, inside the Rangashala, in the presence of numerous lusty royal and affluent upper-class men, all drunkards, another episode of disrobing will begin. Centering around one or the other maid, the disrobing will continue as an ugly game, as a regular ritual of the festive nights for years and centuries to come. These repeated disrobing *Parbas* will not be penned down by anyone, by any *mahakavi*. This will remain as an Andhika Parv—a tale which appears and disappears in the darkness of the night.

Epilogue

The night when Nidalu's daughter Sevudasi entered the entertainment house Rangashala carrying a vessel of liquor, a meditative sage far away in a deep jungle attained a strange enlightenment.

The sage, with in-depth knowledge of the prime truth subscribed in the *Sankhyadarshana*, meditated for years seeking enlightenment of a newer horizon. Going beyond all visible evidence, following all existing and non-existing wisdom, he attained the power of projecting his vision into the past, present and future. He had become the omniscient seer with prophetic vision for the future beyond centuries. To try out his power he closed his eyes and started a psychic journey within. As he went into the Samadhi, a few scenes unfolded before his eyes.

Scene 1: A gigantic Rangashala lit up with strings of rainbow-coloured lamps of some yet un-invented light of florescence; the Rangashala shines like a thousand moons. Seated in them are more than a hundred royal men, merchants, generals and officials of the royal court on thrones. On a raised platform is a group of scantily clad apsaras revealing their full body except for the tips of their two round *gumadaon*, the bosom, and the *pipalapatra*-like mound below the navel. They are walking in a row on a platform built in the middle of that hall and those sitting in the thrones are devouring each movement of those gyrating beauties with their eyes.

Scene 2: Yet another big hall. In that hall are the broken pieces of some ruins, stacked neatly in rows. Those remains have seemingly been collected from various places over thousands of years. Amidst them is an idol of a naked woman in a triangular poster, one of her legs wrapped around a tree and her raised hand holding a branch. The saint is pleasantly surprised to see that standing in front of that beautiful sculpture is a teacher and a group of pupils discussing the probable history of that nude idol.

Then the vision of the yogi shifted to another corner of the globe.

Scene 3: The road of a town with a huge gathering of people. A few carrying arms are disrupting the peace and order. The backdrop turns utterly chaotic as a procession of protesting people go anarchic. A young girl in her prime, who reminds him of the Yakshi figurine, starts running in fear, gets lost and looks for a way to escape. Three youths catch hold of that dusky Adivasi woman and strip her completely naked. Before some young man with a conscience can rush to the woman and cover her nakedness, the unthinkable happens. A few divine tools making a click-click sound captures the disrobed figure. From one instrument to another, the scene gets transmitted to thousands of similar instruments and another highly complicated tool, like the divine vision of Sanjay, which can project any incident taking place anywhere in this Brahmanda, projects that scene into every household in this world. A thousand times the young woman gets stripped. The drama of disrobing is enjoyed by millions of eyes. The entire world becomes the royal court of Hastinapur.

Though the second scene brought a ray of *ananda*—delight and calm—the first and third scenes fills the yogi's mind with intense despair. This means the world will not change even thousands of years hence. Filled with bitterness, while he was getting ready for the return journey, he saw yet another unique scene.

Scene 4: The household of a lord, probably a preacher guru with stacks of books in rows. In a corner of the house, a dasi is washing a few utensils. Completing her chores, she goes back to a room, picks up a pen and starts writing. To his utter amazement, the yogi discovers that it is a chapter of her autobiography. The yogi gazes at that radiant face of the resolute, new female *vedavyasi* named Baby Halyadhar with immense fascination.

'A phase of darkness will come with every era, but amidst that illusive darkness, a flash of consciousness and a voice of light will always burn to dispel that darkness—be it in the form of a verse, a fable, an idol or whatever form or shape it can find.' Thus spoke the yogi with a subtle smile and started upon his return journey. By the time he reached back it was time for the morning goddess to appear, the Usha, and lo and behold, our Sevudasi had come out as an Usha, as she composed her first oral verse stepping out of the Rangashala:

You think you have made me the slave,
You can enslave my body but,
Can you enchain my spirit and my being?
I am free . . .
So free am I . . . so gloriously free.

**Written in protest against the disrobing of Lakshmi Urang, an Adivasi woman in the streets of Beltola, Guwahati, Assam in 2007 and inspired by the famous poem from the Therīgāthā, or *Songs of the Nuns*, (sixth century BCE) originally written in the Pali language. Thanks also to Dr Sanjib Sahoo for provoking me to write this story on the evening of that disrobing incident.

Acknowledgements

My heartfelt gratitude to these warm and wonderful people without whom this book would have not been possible:

Sathya Saran, Milee Ashwarya, Elizabeth Kuruvilla, Vidushi Khera, Nicholas Rixon, Saloni Mital, Aditi Shenoy, Pinaki Sarkar, Sanghamitra S. Kalita, K. Satchidanandan, Ajitabh Hazarika and, last but not the least, my dear friend Parbina Rashid.

And I am incredibly blessed to have these beautiful people around me. The writer I am today is as much a result of their unconditional support and confidence in me as it is of my drive and passion: Late Khudindranath Kandali, Tarulata Kandali, Mallika Kandali, Monimala Kandali, Dhruvarka Deka, Deeptangshu Das, Arindam Borkataki, Anindita Goswami, Wriju Gohain, Sangeeta Modi, Sonika Sankhyaan, Nabajit Deory and Swapnarka (Rong).